I0550507

The Power
Of Love

Second Edition

Jenny Leigh Jones

Flashover Press

FLASHOVER PRESS

This book is a work of fiction. Names, characters, places, and incidents are either products of the author's imagination or are used fictitiously. Any resemblance to actual events or locales or persons, living or dead, is entirely coincidental.

ISBN: 0615972756
ISBN: 978-1311853943 (ebook)
ISBN: 978-0615972756 (paperback)

DEDICATION

This book is dedicated to all the people in my life who have encouraged and inspired me to write this novel. To my husband who's put up with me and who's been patient with me always writing. My mother and sister who read my book to tell me what they really thought. My grandmother, who not only read my book, but spent hours with a highlighter to point out my every mistake. And to my good friends, Andrea and Paula, who not only read my book while I was writing it, but helped me make it better.

There are several others who have given me encouragement and who believed in me - and you know who you are. I dedicate this book to you.

The second edition of this book is dedicated to the man who made it happen! It would still be gathering dust on a shelf if it weren't for him.

Thank you all!

CONTENTS

CHAPTER 1

As the whole world seemed not to see her, Leela rushed down Main Street. She was late for work again and Sammy was going to fire her if she was late. In the six weeks Leela had worked at the diner she was late at least once a week. Sammy had understood at first but she was now losing her patience.

"Doctor's appointment or not," Sammy told her the last time, "I cannot let you get away with being late if all my other waitresses have to be on time."

Waiting tables at the diner wasn't easy work. She was on her feet at least eight hours a day. She would nearly pass out by the end of her shift, and would struggle to make her way home to the one-room apartment she rented for almost nothing. It wasn't a pretty room or a room to entertain in, but Leela had no friends - especially no boyfriends. She wasn't exactly what most people called pretty and she was too shy to actually talk to a guy anyway.

Leela shuffled her way through the crowds of people waiting for the bus. They were dressed in spring clothes. It was a warm day for March. She was two blocks away from the diner and it was exactly eight o'clock. That meant she was going to be late. She had to stop by the clinic earlier in the morning to have blood work done. She had been there at exactly seven and figured that would give her plenty of time for the vampires to take her blood and still get to work on time. Apparently that was what everyone else was thinking too, because the clinic was packed.

As Leela rushed through the door of the diner, Ashley, another waitress, walked up to her.

"Don't worry, Leela," Ashley said under her breath, "she hasn't been out of the bathroom all morning and doesn't know you're late." Leela quickly thanked her and put on her apron. Today was going to be a long day; work was always harder after she had her blood taken. Leela looked around the diner and saw there were four waitresses working today, which only gave her seven tables. Usually Sammy staffed two waitresses but Mondays were a big day at the diner so she double staffed. Monday was discount day, and they gave discounts to almost everyone- doctors, lawyers, and law enforcement agencies. Leela was pouring coffee to an elderly couple at one of her tables when Sammy finally made an appearance at the counter, smiling from ear to ear.

"Good morning, Leela!" she exclaimed. Leela had no idea why she was in such a good mood since Ashley had told her that she hadn't left the bathroom all morning. "I have some good news. Jake and I are going to have a baby!" Sammy said, laughing. Jake and Sammy had been married for five years and had tried all of those years to get pregnant, and it had finally happened.

"Congrats!" Leela said back as enthusiastic as she could. Leela was happy for Sammy but she didn't feel so good. She was having dizzy spells off and on and just figured it was due to having blood work done earlier in the morning. Not to mention that since Leela had only worked there a little over a month she didn't really feel all that close to Sammy, but the other waitresses that had worked there for years were hugging her and congratulating her.

The morning went by at a fast pace for Leela. Her

seven tables were constantly filled with doctors and she stayed very busy. Around noon Leela felt like she could take it no longer, her head was pounding and her knees felt weak.

"Sammy, can I take lunch now?" Leela was starting to look a little pale so Sammy nodded yes.

"Leela, are you all right?" Leela hadn't told anyone at the diner about her condition.

"Yeah, Sammy," Leela lied. "Just real tired today for some reason."

Leela walked to the back of the diner where the break room was and took off her apron and hair net. Leela had thirty minutes and didn't feel much like eating, so she just laid her head on the table and closed her eyes.

"Leela, wake up!"

Leela jumped up and realized she was sleeping - Ashley was shaking her. Her lunch was over and Sammy was asking about her. Leela stood up and went to reach for her apron and she fell, her legs just gave out and her knees buckled. Ashley ran over to her and grabbed her arm.

"Oh my, Leela, are you okay?"

Leela felt her cheeks getting red. All the blood in her body, what was left anyway, was rushing to her face. She was so embarrassed and was beginning to panic.

"Yes, I'm sorry," she said as she stood up, this time with the help of Ashley and the chair she was sitting in.

"Maybe you should ask Sammy to go home," Ashley said, worried about her. She was very pale.

"No, I'm fine. Please don't tell Sammy. I need the money so I need to stay."

"Leela, you don't look fine. I'm sure it will be okay if you want to go home, or maybe to a doctor?" Leela shook her head quickly.

"No, Ashley. I've just been tired, that's all. I'm fine. Please, don't tell Sammy."

Ashley hesitated. "Okay." Leela put her apron and hair net back on and headed out toward the front.

The rest of the afternoon went by as fast as the morning. Leela was thankful for that because all she wanted to do was go home and crawl into her bed and sleep. Fifteen minutes before her shift ended a man was seated in her section. She recognized him because he had a face you didn't forget. He ate at the diner often, and was always alone.

Leela was confused, they were not supposed to be seating any more customers in her section since her shift was almost over.

"Paula," Leela asked the waitress who seated the man, "why did you put him in my section? I am leaving soon." Paula gave Leela a warm smile. "He asked for you, honey," she said in a teasing voice. "Now go introduce yourself."

Leela felt herself blushing for the second time that day. *He asked for me?* She thought to herself. Leela was shocked, no one had ever requested her before. Most of the time she had to remind herself to smile and be friendly. Leela was almost too nervous to wait on him, but Paula gave her a friendly shove and Leela started moving toward him.

He was a handsome man, possibly in his early thirties with sandy blond hair perfectly groomed - and crystal blue eyes that seemed to be staring right into hers. He wasn't thin but wasn't heavy either. He looked like he worked out but wasn't obsessed with it. He had a slight tan that made him look very natural, but not overly tan like most people in town. She had to admit he was very handsome.

"Hi," Leela said in barely a whisper. "I'm Leela and I'm going to be your waitress." She was nervous. "Can I get you some coffee?" she asked. The man smiled.

"Nice to meet you, Leela. My name is Clay. Clay Warner, and yes, I would like some coffee. But decaf." Leela poured him a cup of decaffeinated coffee.

"Anything to eat today?" she asked. "Our special is the meat loaf." Clay wrinkled up his nose and made a funny face.

"Oh no you don't, Leela. You guys got me on the meat

loaf last time I was here, and that is when I figured you had to put it on special to get anyone to order it." He was laughing as he said it and Leela cracked a smile. He was joking with her.

"Actually, Leela," Clay started, "I was hoping to see if you wanted to get some dinner with me tonight, somewhere that you didn't have to serve it. Then maybe a movie?"

Leela froze. This man was asking her out and she couldn't understand why. Leela was practically invisible to most men in this town and she knew she was not all that attractive with plain brown hair and thick glasses worn over her hazel eyes. She was skinny as a rail and - let's face it - didn't have a womanly figure.

"Well?" Clay asked again. He noticed the shocked look on her face. "I've been in here a lot lately and I see how hard you work. Let me take you out, I promise I won't bite." he said, laughing.

"Actually, I am really tired tonight," Leela said as calmly as she could.

Clay looked hurt for a moment, then quickly recovered. "Well, what about tomorrow night?" Leela just looked at him. She couldn't get close to anyone, and no one even wanted to get close to her because she made sure of it.

"Look, Clay," she said, "I really appreciate your offer, but I really can't."

Clay laid two dollars down on the table and got up.

"Well, Leela, I'll leave you alone tonight. However, I really want to take you out so, I will be back tomorrow to ask again." With a grin he laid a business card down on the table and walked through the door. He was gone.

Leela just stood there for a moment before realizing the other three waitresses as well as Sammy standing behind the counter, looking at her in amazement. They couldn't believe she turned him down. As quickly as she could she took off her apron and hair net and made her way to the time clock. By five after five she was walking down Main Street on her way home.

Chapter 2

That night after a long hot shower Leela sat on her second-hand couch eating a frozen TV dinner. She couldn't believe that man had asked her out. *What did he say his name was, Clay something?* She was now regretting not picking up the business card he left. *Oh well*, she thought. It's not like she would have gone out anyway. She didn't do things like that.

Leela was twenty-six years old and lived alone, and she had no family. Her mother and father were both dead. She did have a brother named Alex, but they hadn't spoken in six years. He was five years her senior and had left home before their parents died. She saw him six years ago at the funeral, and not one time since. It was then that Leela decided she needed to get way from her hometown, so she had packed up and moved to this little town in South Carolina. A place where no one knew her, and no one would bother her.

Leela had some pamphlets sitting on the table next to the couch. They had been given to her at the doctor's office two months before, when she was diagnosed with her awful condition. Leela was in denial, and had yet to read any of the tiny booklets. She figured if she didn't read about her condition it might just go away. She didn't even know half the symptoms from it, and was not mentally prepared to find out yet.

She picked one up and scanned the words on the glossy front, but then quickly set it aside. "I couldn't care less if I die from this, but I don't want to read about it," she muttered to her empty living room.

Resting on the very same table was an old family photo, and Leela picked it up. It had been taken while she was in high school, and was the only picture she could remember seeing with her mom, dad, brother, and her all in it. They had been a happy family, and she missed her parents so much. Alex was always the popular one in school being the handsome and cool type, and Leela had been his polar opposite. Despite their obvious differences the two had gotten along well as children.

Alex had taken their parent's death hard, and shortly after the house fire that had claimed their lives, he had simply stopped making contact with Leela. He had moved to Virginia, and having no one left Leela had gone to South Carolina. For six long years she hadn't heard from her estranged brother, so she was surprised when a letter had arrived in the mail only a few days previous.

As she sat staring at her old family picture she contemplated the letter from her brother. Alex had met a woman and become engaged, and he and his fiancée Laura were soon to be married. In the letter he apologized for all the distance he had forced between them and then asked her to attend the wedding. Leela was filled with mixed emotions. The brother who'd abandoned her was getting married while she would very likely be a spinster for the rest of her life, a life that could very well be cut short due to her condition.

Despite his long absence from her life she couldn't help but be happy for her brother. After all, six years ago he was her best friend, and now she had no one. Sometimes she resented him for leaving her all alone, he had always known she was the shy type and very rarely made any friends. Her one true friend had left her to mourn their parents alone.

As she put down the picture, her phone rang. With a sigh she reached for the handset, no one ever called her unless it was the diner needing her to pick up an extra shift.

"Hello?" she answered.

"Leela?" It took her a moment to recognize the voice on the other end of the line, and with a bit of shock she realized it was Alex.

Her estranged brother "Al." It was the first time in years she had heard his voice, but she knew instantly who it was. "Leela, how are you?"

She could tell he felt awkward calling her. "I'm okay, Alex, how are you?"

There was a pause,

"Lee, I'm fine. Did you get my letter?" Leela smiled to herself.

"Yeah, congrats!" Leela felt a twinge of pain as she said it. Everyone had moved forward in life but her.

"Leela, the wedding is going to be in South Carolina because that is where Laura's family is from. Actually, we will be in the same town where you live. Isn't that crazy? Well, we are coming up next weekend to see her folks, and I was hoping to see you and introduce you to Laura."

Leela felt panic rise up in her chest. "Alex, that is great. I'd love to see you." Alex could tell Leela was hesitant.

"Look, Leela," he started. "I am really sorry about the last couple years. I should have called. I met Laura a year ago and when she found out I had a sister, well, she made me realize how insensitive I have been. It was just as hard on you as it was on me. Are you doing okay?"

Leela had tears in her eyes. "I'm doing okay, Al. I can't wait to see you and meet Laura." They talked for a few more minutes about how their lives were going, and then hung up. Alex promised to call at the end of the week before they left, and promised to keep in touch this time.

Leela felt emotion rise in her chest as she lay on her couch staring at the family portrait again. She should have been mad. She should have yelled at him, but she couldn't. She loved him and was happy he had called. And she meant it when she said she couldn't wait to see him.

Alex had told her that he had finished law school and was working for a law firm in Virginia, and he was doing well. Laura was a secretary for one of his friends at the firm, and that was how the two had met. She had no brothers or sisters, but her folks lived in the same town as Leela lived now. *That's so odd*, she thought to herself. Leela fell asleep on the old couch still clutching the picture to her chest.

When Leela woke up to her alarm at six-thirty, she realized she was still holding the picture. Had the call from Alex been a dream? She couldn't believe he actually called. She had wanted to call him so many times over the years when she was depressed and needed someone to talk to - but never did. Now, he had finally called her. She felt a bit weak as she got dressed for work, but excited at the same time. She was actually going to get to see her brother this weekend.

Then she felt disappointed. *He is doing so well*, she thought, *and look at me. I am a waitress living in a one-bedroom apartment.* Then she realized that she didn't care if she didn't have any accomplishments to show, she didn't need any. All she had was herself and she didn't need anyone else.

As Leela walked through the doors of the diner she glanced at her watch. It was seven forty-five and she was early. Sammy would be shocked. She had decided when she left her home that she was going to have a good day today. Things were looking up, her brother was coming to visit and she was excited. Over at the counter her co-worker Ashley was sitting on a stool, grinning impishly.

"Hey, Leela, you left last night without taking Mr. Right's number."

"What in the world are you talking about, Ash?" Leela was confused.

"Clay Warner?" Ashley said in a teasing voice. Leela stopped and looked at Ashley.

"Oh him," she said, laughing. "I had forgotten." Ashley began laughing as well.

"Well here," she said, putting the business card in the pocket of Leela's apron. "Here is his number. *Call him.*" Leela laughed and shook her head.

"That's okay, Ash, why don't you go out with him?" Ashley couldn't believe that Leela wasn't interested in this man, he was good looking and she had never heard Leela talk about a boyfriend before.

Ashley decided to push her. She wanted to find out more about Leela. She had worked with her for over a month now and Leela refused to let Ashley get close.

"Leela, why don't you like him?"

"Okay, fine!" Leela said, sensing that Ashley wanted the truth. "Look at me, Ashley. I am not pretty. Why would anyone want to go out with me?"

Ashley was shocked. *Leela could be pretty*, she thought to herself.

"Oh you are so full of it!" she shot back. "Leela, come with me after work to my place." Leela felt anxiety creeping in. Why would Ashley want her to go to her place? She felt that anxiety every time someone tried to get close to her. She had let no one into her life her since her parents died and her brother disappeared. She was afraid to get hurt, and Ashley could clearly see the hesitation on Leela's face.

"Come on, Leela, I went to beauty school a few years ago. I want to show you that you could be gorgeous." Leela blushed, and then hung her head.

"Ashley, why are you being so nice to me?" Ashley looked hurt.

"Leela, I like you. I just want to be your friend." Leela finally gave in.

"Okay, fine."

Ashley smiled at this small victory and they both went to work. All day long Leela kept thinking about her brother and his new wife to be. People in this town were nice and she hoped Laura would be, too. However, she had lived here for a while and no one had wanted to befriend her the way Ashley seemed to. Leela didn't pull away, though. She figured that she could use at least one friend. What's the harm?

At four o'clock Leela was talking to Ashley at the counter when Clay Warner walked through the door. Leela had her back to him and had no clue he was there until Ashley kicked her.

"Leela, Prince Charming is back." Leela was confused at first and then she heard his voice behind her.

"Hello, ladies." Leela turned around and was face to face with him.

She hadn't realized how tall he was yesterday while he sat at her table, and she realized he had to be at least six feet tall.

"Good afternoon," Leela said back. Ashley was trying not to laugh. Leela kept waiting for him to sit down, but he just kept standing there. "Can I get you a menu?" she asked.

Clay smiled. He had a smile that melted a girl's heart. "Actually, Leela, I don't have time today. I just wanted to stop in and see if you would have dinner tomorrow night?" Leela was blushing again, but before she could decline Ashley stepped up.

"She would love to!" she exclaimed. Leela looked at Ashley with horror. She was in shock and she couldn't make anything come out of her mouth even though she was trying to tell him she couldn't.

"Great!" he said. "I'll pick you up here at five tomorrow, then." With that he turned and walked out the door, before Leela could even catch her voice. Ashley was beaming from ear to ear as Leela looked at her in amazement.

"I can't believe you told him I would go out with him!" she cried, trying not to laugh. She wanted to be mad at Ashley but she couldn't. Ashley was laughing herself.

"Just wait until I make you beautiful!"

Chapter 3

As their shift ended and the two night waitresses started waiting tables, Ashley and Leela walked down Main Street together. Ashley promised to give Leela the confidence to go out with hunk Clay Warner the next evening. They were joking and laughing as they walked. Leela hadn't felt like this since she was in high school. To her surprise she realized that Ashley only lived two blocks from her apartment. Ashley's apartment was a cozy two-bedroom above an antique shop off Main. As Ashley was giving Leela the tour of the place, Leela was surprised to find that the second bedroom had toy cars and trains in it.

"And this," Ashley said, "Is my son Ryan's room." Leela looked at her in amazement, she had no idea Ashley had any kids. Ashley was her age - give or take a year - and had never mentioned Ryan. "Ryan is five now. He is staying with his father this week." Ashley could tell Leela was shocked. "I had just turned twenty-one and his father bolted before Ryan was even born. But he still sees him on a regular basis. He's a good father and is married with another son that's four." Leela felt sorry for Ashley.

"Wow, Ash," Leela said. "I had no idea you had any kids." Ashley didn't want Leela to feel sorry for her. She had a good life and didn't struggle.

"We do okay." Then they walked back into the living room.

Within an hour Leela and Ashley seemed to be best friends and Leela felt like she could open up to her. She told her everything about herself, about her parents and her brother, everything except the condition. In such a short time they seemed to know each other's life stories. Ashley told Leela she wanted to cut and highlight her hair and Leela said okay, even though she was nervous. They ordered a pizza and for the first time in years Leela was having fun.

Around eight o'clock Ashley stood back, admiring her work. She had given Leela a haircut, style and highlights. She put makeup on her and took off her glasses after Leela said she had a pair of contacts at her apartment that she rarely used. Ashley made her promise to wear them.

After all was said and done, Leela looked gorgeous. She was shocked when she looked in the mirror and almost didn't recognize herself. She smiled a grin at Ashley.

"Why are you waiting tables when you have such a talent of making people pretty?" Ashley was pleased with her work.

"Well, Ryan happened. When I got pregnant I dropped out of Beauty College and never went back." Leela felt sorry for her. Ashley could tell and quickly reassured her. "Leela, Ryan is the best thing that ever happened to me." and Leela could tell she meant it. Leela thanked her for all the wonderful things she had done for her, and Ashley replied with a hug. Leela was getting ready to leave when Ashley said to her, "You were always beautiful, Leela. You just didn't know it."

As Leela walked the two blocks to her apartment, she stood tall. She felt beautiful and for the first time in years she felt like she was somebody and not just the invisible girl who walked in the shadows of everyone else. When she got home she found her contacts and puts them in. She saw herself more clearly than she had in a long time, and what she saw was beautiful. All her life she wanted to feel pretty and now she did. Her hair was cute and shiny with its new highlights and her face glowed under the makeup Ashley had carefully applied.

Then she remembered that she had a date tomorrow

night. For the first time in, well ever, she had a date with a very handsome man. What would she wear? She didn't she had anything that would suit her look until she remembered a dress she had bought on a clearance rack two years before. It had looked nice, but she had never had a reason to wear it.

Leela took the deep purple dress out of the back of the closet and placed it on the bed. Then she pulled out a pair of strappy black shoes that she had bought at the same time and placed them next to the dress.

As Leela looked at herself in the mirror she realized just how much she liked her new hair cut. She loved the layers and the color Ashley had put in it. They brought out her eyes, which now were not hiding behind those thick lenses she required.

"Wow!" she just kept saying to herself.

Leela decided to try the dress on and make sure it fit right. As she took her work apron off, something fell out of it and slid under her bed. When she went to pick it up, she realized it was Clay Warner's business card. That made her laugh to herself. "I have a date with a 'computer programmer,'" she read off the business card. She was so excited. She hadn't stopped smiling since she got to Ashley's.

For the first time in years, Leela felt like she had a friend. She set Clay's business card on the table by her bed and pulled off her blouse she wore under the apron. Then she unbuttoned her black skirt and let it fall down to the floor. Leela looked at he small frame in the mirror, she had tried to gain weight once but it just didn't work. She was so thin. The last time she had a doctor's appointment the scale had told her she weighed only 105 pounds. *How could any man find me attractive*, she thought as she studied herself. *I'm lacking the one thing they notice first. Big Boobs!* Leela was barely a B cup. Her bra size was 32 B and she wished it were more like 34 D.

Leela pulled the dress on over her head and it fell into

place like it was meant to be there, then she put the strappy shoes on. When Leela looked back in the mirror she was amazed. In a matter of only three short hours she had been transformed. The dress fit her perfectly, and actually accentuated her bust, allowing her more ample cleavage than she was accustomed to. Leela then hurried up and got out of the dress and hung it back up so it didn't get wrinkled, then she took a long hot bath.

Leela lay in bed that night not able to fall asleep. It was ten o'clock and she was so excited that she didn't want to stay still so she decided to get up and make some hot chocolate. That is what her mom used to make her when she couldn't sleep as a child.

As she climbed out of bed she caught a glimpse of the business card she had laid there two hours before, and for a moment she gazed at the small picture next to his name and number. Clay Warner was a very handsome man. He was going to pick her up at 5, after her shift tomorrow evening and she could hardly wait.

Chapter 4

On Wednesday the diner was slow all day. Ashley and Leela spent most of the day sitting at the counter and talking. Ashley told Leela all about Ryan and Leela promised to come by that weekend and meet him. If you hadn't known better you would have thought the two of them had been friends forever. Sammy took note of the girl's new-found friendship on several occasions throughout the day. She was happy though, Leela was such a nice girl and Sammy hated seeing her so lonely all the time. She was also surprised and impressed that Leela had actually agreed to go out with this man who kept coming in the diner just to see her. She made it a point to compliment Leela's hair more than once throughout the day.

At quarter till five Leela was panicking. She was convinced that all this was a horrible trick and that Clay wasn't coming to pick her up at all. Just as she was venting to Ashley for the tenth time that day he walked the object of her frustrations walked in. Ashley kicked Leela under the counter and Leela turned around and faced him.

"Wow, Leela, you look great!" he said right away.

"Thanks!" Leela beamed back. Clay was dressed in a nice suit, which made Leela happy because as soon as her shift ended she was going to change into the dress she had brought from home.

"Leela, we're slow. Go ahead and clock out." Sammy was letting her loose.

"Great," Clay said. "Are you ready to go then?" Leela

looked at him in horror.

"I'm not wearing this out. I want to change first okay?" Clay took a step back like he was shocked.

"You look so beautiful now, dear, but if you must, you may." Leela laughed as she ran back to the break room to change into her dress.

It took all of five minutes for Leela to get dressed and Ashley to put the finishing touches on her hair. When all was said and done Ashley told her she was a knock out!

When Leela walked back into the front of the diner she felt all eyes on her. Sammy was in awe. Clay's jaw had dropped. A few of the regulars at the diner also stared. After a moment Clay snapped out of it and walked up to Leela.

"Wow, again!"

Leela could tell she had made an impression on him. "Leela, I just don't know what to say. You were pretty before, but you are beautiful now!" Leela felt her face blush red. She was embarrassed. Ashley handed Leela her purse and told her to call her then she walked up to Clay and he put his arm around hers. They walked out of the diner arm in arm.

"Where are we going?" Leela asked Clay.

"Aww, my beauty, it's a surprise. Just sit back and relax." They were in Clay's car. He had a nice car and it looked brand new. Clay leaned over and turned on the radio and Leela heard love songs coming through the speakers.

"Tell me about yourself, Leela," Clay said. Leela felt awkward. After all, she had barely even said two words to this man.

"Well, Clay," she started. "I am twenty-six years old, live alone, and work at the diner." Clay laughed.

"Well, I am glad to hear you live alone. I was afraid you had a boyfriend or something. Are you from here?"

"Actually no, I am from Indiana. I moved here about six years ago. What about you?" she asked back.

"Well, I have lived in this little old town my whole life. And as you can hopefully see, I also live alone." Leela smiled. She was starting to feel a little more comfortable with him.

He was just telling her about his sister when they pulled up in front of a really nice restaurant called South Steak House. Leela had never eaten there before as it was too expensive for her salary at the diner.

"Here we are," Clay said as he parked the car. "Is this place okay?" Leela almost laughed.

"Of course!" she said.

They were seated almost immediately when they entered the place. While they waited for their food they talked about everything they could think of. Leela was surprised how at ease she felt with him and felt he was a true gentleman.

They were sipping their wine when Clay said, "You know, Leela, I have been going past the diner my whole life and never could bring myself to eat there. In the last month though I have eaten there three days a week for lunch." That surprised her. She knew he came in there quite regularly but she didn't realize it was that often, and she hadn't realized it was just since she started. Leela felt herself blush again, she embarrassed easily.

"Why me?" she finally asked the question she had been wondering.

"Leela, you are so sweet, so pure. I look into your eyes and I see pain. I want to be the one to make your eyes dance and smile. The first time I saw you, I immediately knew I had to be with you. You had tears in your eyes and all I wanted to do was comfort you, but you never let me get near you."

Leela had tears in her eyes as he spoke those words. She had no idea he had seen that deep into her soul and suddenly she remembered the first time she saw him. It was the day of her worst doctor's appointment and although she had cried all day long, she still had to work.

"Clay, I'm sorry I upset you." But as she said that he knew there was more to it. He could tell he hadn't earned the right to know what that was yet, but in time he was determined to have this girl. The rest of the night was like a scene out of a fairy tale. Clay had said all the right things to Leela, and she was apparently everything he had hoped because he was on cloud nine all evening. When it came time and the waiter brought the check, Leela couldn't believe it was almost eight o'clock.

"Leela, I know this is the first time we've ever gone out but I feel like I've known you for an eternity." Leela knew exactly what he meant. But he wanted to hold back these feelings until she got to know him more. She had never been in love before, and she was afraid of being hurt by. She had been so afraid, in fact, that she had never let herself even agree to dinner with someone before.

"Clay, I had a wonderful time tonight, too." She hoped she hadn't hurt him by not returning his sentiment.

"Does it have to end here?" he asked. Leela didn't know what to say. If he wanted to go do something else like a movie, she would be okay, but she was afraid he meant something else. She wasn't prepared for that.

"I do have to work early tomorrow but what do you have in mind?" Clay could tell she was conflicted by his question. He didn't want to in any way run her off. It had been such a lovely evening so far.

"How about a romantic walk down the ocean."

He was so sweet, and that made her smile.

"That sounds nice," she said in a low voice.

Clay paid their check and they walked to the car hand in hand. They only had to drive a short distance until they came to a secluded beach. Before they got out of the car, Clay took off his shoes and rolled up his pant legs. Leela realized she couldn't walk in the sand in heels so she, too, took off her black strappy shoes. Then he told her to stay put and he got out of the car and walked around to the other side.

As he opened her door for her the moonlight was shining down on her face and he, for the first time, saw a beauty he hadn't before. She was glowing. Maybe it was the dinner but he felt that he was already falling in love with her. After all, he had been watching her for a month before he found the nerve to ask her out.

They were almost to the waterfront when Clay laid a hand on Leela's arm and stopped her. Raising his hands to her shoulders he gently turned her to face him.

"Leela, I have been waiting for a month to get the chance to take you out."

Leela didn't know what to say. She was falling fast. She never in a million years thought tonight would affect her the way it had. She was afraid but curious as well. She thought she might be letting herself get too close.

When Leela didn't respond to his comment he decided to kiss her and as he moved closer he realized she was slowly moving away. And as he looked in her eyes he saw a pain that hadn't been there before.

"I'm sorry," he said and slowly turned away. Leela didn't know what to say or do. She was afraid to get too close. She still hadn't told him about her condition and hadn't really planned on having to tell anyone about it. She sensed that he wanted to be close and she didn't know what to do. If she got close to him and he left her, she'd be hurt. But if she got close to him and the condition got her, he'd be hurt. She didn't want it either way. He sensed something was wrong and he also sensed she didn't want to discuss it. So he took her hand and they walked in silence down the beach, hand in hand.

Their seaside walk eventually led them back to the car, and although neither had spoken during the course of the walk, the quiet was not an uncomfortable. As Clay put his shoes back on Leela could tell she had already hurt him. It wasn't intentional, but she didn't see any reason to take it any further with such a dark cloud looming over them. It seemed only a few minutes later they were pulling to the curb in front of her apartment and he was walking her to the her door.

"I had a great time," Leela said. Clay smiled and her heart melted.

"I did, too. Can I see you again?" Leela wanted to say yes but she knew that it wasn't a good idea.

"We'll see," she said, instead of no. She didn't want to let him down so soon, and he seemed to read her mind as he nodded, thinking she was trying to let him down gently. Afraid he was going to try to kiss her again she decided to beat him to it. She reached up and stood on her tiptoes to kiss him chastely on his cheek, and as she did he slid his hands about her waist and turned into her kiss. Before she knew it his lips had met hers and he was slowly kissing her.

She tried to resist at first but she felt an overpowering urge, and she kissed him back with more passion than she had meant to. It seemed like forever before Clay finally pulled away. She felt weak in the knees and experienced a feeling she herself had never felt before. Her whole body was tingling and she had an aching need to feel his body against hers.

"Leela?" Clay asked as he stood there staring into her eyes. Leela didn't answer with words but instead with her eyes. "Do you want me to leave now?" he asked, hoping she would say no while at the same time not wanting to ruin anything, either. He knew that she was frightened by something earlier at the beach and he didn't want to scare her away. He didn't want just one night with her - he wanted a lifetime!

She still hadn't answered him because she didn't know what to say, she wanted to feel him close to her. After the kiss she had had let go of all the worries she had only an hour before. She was about to ask him in when he kissed her again, not with as much passion but with much more meaning. He pulled away after only a moment and looked into her eyes. What he saw in those eyes told him he could have her right now if he wanted.

"Leela, I am going to go now."

She was shocked. She was prepared to let him in not only to her apartment, but her life.

"But," she started to say.

"Leela, I don't want to ruin a good thing." She understood perfectly what he was saying and as he turned away from her all she could do was stare. When he got to his car he turned and their eyes locked. "I think I love you," he said. Then he got into his car and drove away.

Leela couldn't move. *Did he just say? Yes, I think he did,* she thought. And she realized after a few minutes she was still on her porch. She let herself in and walked inside. In the living room she took off her shoes and stripped out of her dress. It was then she saw the light on her answering machine blinking. Clay's last words were on her mind as she pushed the play button.

"Leela, it's Alex. Plans have changed and we'll be in tomorrow. Laura got a few extra days off work so we can spend more time together. I'll call you tomorrow night when we get to Laura's parents' house." And then it was done.

Leela lay in bed that night but again couldn't fall asleep. She still had the tingling feeling throughout her body and she kept thinking about the kiss. Could she love him, too? It was too insane a thought; she had only just met him. She finally drifted off to sleep with the image of Clay in her head.

Chapter 5

The next morning at the diner was a busy one. Ashley was dying to hear the details of the evening but the crowd just wouldn't allow it. She could tell it went well by the constant smile on Leela's face and even Sammy had commented to Ashley that Leela seemed different.

Leela was on a natural high. She had had a wonderful time the night before, but it left her confused. He had said he loved her, didn't he? And she thought she could be in love with him in the future. She had only gone out with him once, so how was she to know if he was the one? She was so preoccupied with her thoughts of the previous night that she hadn't noticed a big bouquet of flowers being delivered to the counter.

"Hey, Lee!" she heard Ashley yell. She looked up. "For you!" As Leela walked to the counter she saw the beautiful flowers. They were all spring blooms and every flower was perfect. There wasn't a flawed petal in the bunch. There was a card that read:

To my Love. I had a wonderful time and I hope you enjoyed it as well. I cannot hold feelings as strong as mine back any longer. I will not bother you if you don't want to be bothered but you have my number.

Call me tonight after work if you will see me again. If you won't see me, my heart will break. Don't deny yourself love. Because that is all I want to give you.

Clay

"Holy cow, Leela!" Ashley proclaimed. She had been reading the note over Leela's shoulder. "What are you going to do?" Leela had explained her dilemma to Ashley over lunch. Now she was even more conflicted. He had put the ball in her court and she had to call him, because if she didn't he would think she didn't want to see him again. She very much did, although she wasn't sure if she should. Ashley repeatedly told her she was a fool for not letting things go with the flow on the date, but then Leela hadn't told Ashley about her condition either.

"My brother is coming in tonight," Leela said, trying to change the subject before she got any deeper. Ashley could tell what she was doing, and sensing it was not going any further, she went along with it.

"Oh really, I thought they weren't coming in until Saturday?"

"I just had a message last night that they would be here tonight. By the way, you've lived here all your life. Do you know anyone by the name of Laura? Maybe in her early thirties, who moved away?" Leela assumed someone here should know her, since this was her future sister-in-law's hometown.

"Actually, Leela, do you know her last name? There was this one girl, obviously older than me, that used to date my cousin. Her parents do still live here so maybe that's her. If it is, though, Leela, she is awful. She has been around." Leela made a horrible face. If that was Alex's new wife to be, she would die.

"Hey Ashley, since Ryan will be gone until Saturday do you want to come over tonight?" Leela didn't really feel like being alone.

"Aren't you going to call Mr. Wonderful?" Ashley asked, shocked. *Here we go again,* Leela thought. Ashley would never understand how Leela felt. Even if she knew about the condition she couldn't possibly understand.

"Ash, I really shouldn't." Leela was hoping to leave it there but it didn't look like Ashley was going to drop it.

"Leela, he likes you and he gave you a fairy tale date. What more do you want? He wants you!" Leela was shaking her head.

"That's exactly the problem, Ashley. It was a fairy tale date. It wasn't real."

Ashley was getting frustrated. "Actually, Leela, I have to do the grocery shopping tonight. You'll have your brother anyway."

Leela wasn't sure if Ashley was upset or really just had things to do. She needn't have worried, because before she left Ashley gave Leela a big hug and told her she had to do what was best for herself.

Leela had started to walk home when a cab pulled up in front of the diner. "Leela Jacobs?" a man asked as Leela started to walk by the cab. "Why yes?" she said.

"This cab is for you, paid for already," he said with a smile. He knew that she had no idea.

"By who?" she asked.

"Don't know," the cab driver said, trying not to smile. Whoever paid for the cab had given him a generous tip to stay anonymous. Leela knew it must have been Clay. He obviously didn't want Leela walking home alone so he had sent a cab.

"Well, okay," she said and climbed in the back of the yellow car.

As she settled herself in she saw a little box lying on the seat.

"Also for you," said the driver. Leela was shocked. It looked like a little jewelry box. As the driver took off, she picked up the box and pondered it. Did she want to open it now or wait till she got home? She realized whatever it was she didn't want to have the memory of opening her first gift from Clay in the backseat of a cab. So she put the box in her apron.

Halfway home the suspense was killing her so she pulled the box out and held it in her hand. Only a few more blocks and she would be home, so she could wait. As the cabbie pulled up to the curb at her apartment, she thanked him and jumped out. When she got to her front door she saw an envelope taped to it and she knew if was from Clay. She decided to open the box first and then open the envelope.

She unlocked her door and went inside. Taking off her apron she sat on her couch, staring at the little box. *What is it?* She wondered. She finally screwed up her courage and flipped the velvet lid. She sat on her couch staring at the most beautiful necklace she had ever seen. It was a gold chain with her birthstone set in a charm, all surrounded by diamonds. She didn't even remember telling him when her birthday was and just stared at it in amazement. It was beautiful. Remembering the envelope she carefully pulled the tab up. It read...

To my love. I hope you loved the flowers and I hope you loved the necklace. You should know that I am not trying to buy your love. Just show you mine.

Even if you decide never to see me again the necklace is yours. You have my number.

I will be sitting by the phone in anticipation of your call. With all my love, Clay

This guy was incredible - and maybe even a little scary. He seemed to be coming on pretty strong for a guy who wanted to let her make up her own mind. Then, as she sat there thinking about everything, she noticed the light on her answering machine was blinking. She hit the play button expecting to hear Clay's mesmerizing voice, instead she heard her brother's.

"Hey, Leela, we're in town and staying at the Blue Moon Hotel. My number here is 555-9685 and our room number, just in case you need it, is 5B. We are heading to Laura's mom's house; she lives on Main Street. I'll try you later I guess. Can't wait to see ya, Lee!" Then he had hung up.

Leela was so consumed with the necklace and letter that she had forgotten to see if her brother had called. She picked up the phone and dialed the hotel number. Of course he wasn't in so she left a message with the person at the front check in desk.

"Al, it's Lee, I am home from work now. Call me when you get in because I'll be up late. I work at Sammy's Diner on if you want to come by tomorrow. See ya soon, Al. Tell Laura I can't wait to meet her."

Leela sat on her couch. She had the necklace Clay had gotten her in her hand and she was fingering it and examining every inch of it. What was she going to do? Just as she had decided to call him, the phone rang. *Please let this be Clay*! She thought to herself.

"Hello?" She held her breath.

"Hey, girl! You call him?" Leela wanted to scream. It was Ashley.

"Oh no! I was hoping you were him. He had a cab meet me at the diner tonight, and when I got in there was a small jewelry box. It was a gold necklace with a charm of sapphires and diamonds. " She could hear Ashley gasp at the other end.

"I don't know what to do, Ashley!" Ashley was getting frustrated with Leela again. Why couldn't she just let things go? This man obviously was willing to give her the world. Why wouldn't she take it?

"Leela, why don't you want to be with him? Give me a good solid reason and I'll quit hounding you about it."

Leela was quiet. Should I tell her? "Ashley, I will tell you why because you have become one of my very special friends. I need to tell you something, but not over the phone. In person, please."

Ashley was quiet. She was really wondering what was going on.

"Leela, is your brother in town?" Leela told her that he was, but he was at his fiancée's mother's house. "Do you plan on seeing Clay tonight?" Leela told her she didn't.

"Then, Leela, I'm coming over and you are going to tell me everything you've been holding back." Leela told her okay, and that was the reason why she asked her earlier to come over, Ashley apologized. They hung up after Ashley told Leela she would be there in thirty minutes.

Chapter 6

Leela knew that she just couldn't leave Clay waiting. She was going to call him but she wasn't going to give in. She dialed his number and he picked up on the first ring.

"Hello?" When he answered, he sounded anxious, like he was waiting for a certain call. He was hoping this was her. The phone had rung two minutes before and it had been a telemarketer and it made him furious.

"Clay, it's Leela." Clay felt his heart skip a beat. She had actually called. He was so excited. He was afraid he had scared her off with the cab and the necklace.

"Leela, hi! I am so glad you called. I can't stop thinking about you!" Just hearing his voice brought back the feeling she got when they kissed last night.

"Clay, I have been thinking about it all day, too. Thank you for the flowers and the cab. And the necklace, it was just too much."

Clay was about to pour his heart out to her, tell her how much she was worth each and every one of those gifts when he heard her say: "Clay, this isn't easy for me." Immediately he felt his heart stop.

"No, Leela, don't say it!" She felt like she was breaking his heart. She heard so much pain in his voice.

"Clay, I am not calling to tell you I don't want to see you." She heard him let out a deep breath.

"Oh thank god, Leela, because -" Leela cut him off.

"Clay, I need to think some things out. Until I am sure of the things in my life I can't drag you into it." Clay was confused.

"Leela, I just don't understand." Leela knew he was confused because she was. "Leela, I promise to make you happy." Leela felt a twinge of guilt.

"Oh, Clay, I know you would. And I can't begin to tell you what meeting you has done for me. The truth is...the truth is I need to sort things out and I want you to fit into my life - but I have to make it work. I can not do that until I deal with other issues first." Clay thought he finally understood.

"I didn't realize you had a boyfriend, I'm sorry. If I had known I wouldn't have come on so strong." Leela laughed.

"Clay, there is no man in my life. The truth is you are the first man in my life. You know I'm shy and not all that pretty, at least not until Ashley transformed me the night before our date. I assure you that there is no other man in my life with the exception of my brother that just came into town tonight. Please believe me." He was confused now.

"Okay, Leela, but I just don't understand then."

She knew he wouldn't. "I know, Clay. I'll give you back the necklace, Okay? I don't deserve it for making you wait."

He was almost in tears. "Leela, keep the necklace, and I want you to know that the minute I laid eyes on you over a month ago I thought you were the most beautiful thing I had ever seen. So do not say you aren't, because to me you always have been. When you are ready, I will be here." Then they hung up the phone.

Leela was sitting on the couch with her legs pulled up to her knees when she heard a knock at the door. She knew that was Ashley. As she got up to get the door her legs gave out, and she fell to the floor. Suddenly she was lightheaded and couldn't get up. *Oh no*, she thought. *It's happening again.* She knew that it would be a minute or two before she could get up so she yelled for Ashley to hold on.

Leela's voice was quivering when she yelled. Ashley

opened the door on her own, sensing something was wrong after hearing Leela's quivering voice.

She ran to Leela. "Leela, are you okay?" This was the same thing that had happened at the diner earlier in the week and Ashley was suddenly kicking herself for not finding out what was going on then. "Leela, what is going on?" Leela finally got the strength to get up and she crawled back up to the couch. Ashley went to sit down next to her, and as she set her purse on the coffee table she saw them.

There were three pamphlets. She picked one up and looked at Leela, who nodded yes at the unspoken question. Ashley sat down next to Leela and put her arms around her and together they sat on the couch and cried. Suddenly Ashley understood why Leela was scared. Not only of love, but of death.

"How long have you known?" Ashley asked. Leela told her two months. She told Ashley that she hadn't even read the pamphlets yet past the first page because she just didn't want to know, and then told her about the weekly clinic visits.

"What do the doctors say?" Ashley asked. Leela was hesitant to answer.

"Ashley, I really don't let them tell me much. They tell me it's deadly. I take medicine. But when they try to give me a time frame I refuse to let them. I cannot know if I am going to die, I just can't. Last week when I went he said I was stable, but that could change at any time." Ashley couldn't believe she was hearing this.

"Ashley, do you see now why I am so hesitant with Clay?" Ashley did but she also told Leela she thought she deserved what life brought her. They talked about it for a long time. Around ten o'clock the phone rang. Leela was afraid it was Clay again and she wasn't up to talking, so she let the machine pick it up.

"Leela? It's Alex." Leela jumped up and picked up the phone. "Hey, Alex, I'm here."

Ashley was still sitting on the couch mouthing, "Does he know?"

Leela was frantically shaking her head no.

"Sorry we missed you earlier, Lee. Can I come to the diner and see you tomorrow?" Leela was thrilled with the idea of seeing her brother.

"Oh, Alex, I would love for you to. I take lunch around 11:30. If you can come then I'll have the most time to spend with you." Alex agreed, and they hung up.

"You haven't told your brother yet!" Ashley yelled. Leela looked at Ashley with frustration.

"I just talked to him for the first time in six years. You want me just to come out and say it to him over the phone? You are the only person who knows, Ash. And I would like to keep it that way, okay?" Ashley nodded.

"Aren't you going to tell Clay?" she asked after a moment. Leela thought about that, if she were going to continue seeing him she would have to.

"I don't know if I will have to," she said sadly. Ashley just sighed. They had been through this ten times since Leela let her in on her secret. Ashley obviously thought Leela should continue to see Clay and tell him the truth, but Leela wasn't so sure it was right. Why start a life with someone if you have to end it early? He may not even want a life with her anymore after he finds out. By the time they went around again it was almost ten-thirty. Ashley picked up her purse and gave Leela a hug. She might have been stubborn and hard headed but Ashley was already beginning to think of Leela as a sister. As Ashley was walking home, Leela was lying in bed and crying.

Chapter 7

The morning went by fast as Leela was anticipating her brother's arrival. She noticed today that Ashley was paying a lot of attention to her and she almost regretted telling her, Leela didn't want anyone treating her any differently. She had to adjust to having a friend like Ashley, as she hadn't had a good friend since high school, nearly eight years previous.

At quarter after eleven a man walked through the door and sat at the counter and Ashley walked over to him and asked him what she could get him.

"How about that pretty little waitress over there." Leela happened to be waiting on the table behind him and recognized his voice.

"Alex?" she said as she turned around, and she was suddenly staring into the face of her brother that she hadn't seen in six years. He looked so old and grown up, nothing like how she remembered him. He took a step toward her and she ran up to him and threw her arms around him. They stood there in the middle of the diner hugging with tears in both of their eyes, this was a reunion long over due. Ashley stood by with tears in her eyes, too.

"Go ahead and take your lunch," Sammy told her when she pulled away.

Leela and Alex decided to take a walk. They talked about everything - Leela told Alex about Clay and the most recent developments, and Alex told Leela everything about Laura he could think of. He hadn't brought her because he wanted to get to know Leela again, he had felt so guilty in the last couple years for not contacting her. He had wanted to but didn't think she'd understand, then last year he had realized that she had just as hard of a time with their parents' death as he had. He was horrified to hear Leela spent the last six years alone but was glad to hear in the recent week that she was dating someone and had made a good friend.

He told her she needed to give Clay a chance, and that he had never been happier in his life and he wanted that for her. Her thirty minutes were gone before they knew it, and before she went back to work Alex asked her if she would have dinner with him and Laura tonight. Leela said yes. Before he walked out the door he turned to her and hugged her. "Bring Clay, too," he said.

After the lunch rush Ashley brought Leela the phone.

"Here, I believe your brother told you to do something that I agreed with. Now do it." Leela was shaking. She wanted to call him but she still hadn't told her brother about the condition. If he had known, he might have understood more. When was she going to get the chance to tell him? She didn't think she could to tell him with his fiancée around. She didn't think it was appropriate.

The phone rang three times, and then she got a voice mail. She had dialed the cell phone number that was on his business card. She figured that was the fastest way to reach him, and she decided to leave him a message.

"Clay, hi. It's Leela. I know that last night I told you I needed time to think...but...well...I am having dinner with my brother and his fiancée tonight and I would like you to go, too. I would love to see you again. I'm working at the diner till 4:30, then I'm going to home to change. I'm meeting Alex and Laura at South Steak House at 6:30. I know that it's short notice. I'll understand if you don't want to go but I'd like you to." Then she hung up.

Ashley was disappointed that Leela couldn't get in touch with Clay. She wanted things to work out for her new friend desperately. She had made Leela call Clay's home number as well and leave the same message. If he really meant all he said he'd be there. The first thing Ashley noticed that morning was that Leela was wearing the necklace he gave her. *Good for her*, she thought.

At four-thirty Leela clocked out and walked out of the diner, yelling for Ashley to enjoy her last evening without Ryan. Ashley yelled back for her to do the same. As she started to walk down Main Street she saw Clay standing outside the diner leaning against his car with a single rose in his hand.

"You got my message?" she asked him as they slowly approached each other. Before she could say anything else he handed her the rose and kissed her hard on the mouth. From the window at the diner, Ashley stood smiling. Leela admired Clay's confidence, he wasn't afraid to show her how he felt. Why couldn't she be that brave?

They had two hours before they had to meet her brother and Leela needed to change clothes. She and Clay also needed to talk.

"Clay, I am going to ask you in because we need to have a serious talk. It's only fair to you that we do this before things go any further, Okay? Please, don't try to distract me until after I say what I need to say." Clay, a bit confused, agreed. He was just happy she was letting him in.

When they reached the living room Leela saw she still had her pamphlets sitting on the coffee table. If she moved them now he would see them, so she just left them and hoped he wouldn't look.

"I am going to go change out of this maid stuff." She pulled her apron off and put it on the coffee table over the pamphlets. There, she thought, that will hide them. As she kicked off her shoes she saw his eyes skimming her apartment. A quick check made her confident that there was no other evidence around for him to see.

As she walked into her bedroom she started skimming her closet for something acceptable to wear. She picked out a sweater and skirt that she had hardly worn because she never went anywhere. Since she was always alone she wasn't in the habit of closing her bedroom door, so she had already peeled off her clothes by the time she realized it was open and Clay was standing in the doorway. She was going to get mad and then she realized it was her fault, he must have taken the open door as an invitation. When he realized she saw him he started to blush.

"Leela, you are more beautiful than I imagined." This was not what she had in mind. She wanted to tell him tonight, and instead he was advancing toward her at a speed she couldn't stop. She was going to protest, but before she knew it his lips where on hers and the passion he felt for her in his hands as they gently moved up and down her body.

It was too soon, Leela thought. She had never done this before. She started to panic. Her heart was beating a hundred miles an hour and all she could think of was this man that she was falling for too fast. Clay must have realized how forward he was being and he stopped and looked at her.

"You're not ready yet, are you?" Leela was so thankful he was being so courteous. He had seen the fear in her eyes. Then he realized what she had said the last night they had talked. She had never had a boyfriend before so this might be a first. "I'm sorry, Leela, I just couldn't help myself."

Leela smiled at him and was honest. "Clay, I'm not ready but that doesn't mean I don't want to. Let me figure that out, okay?" Clay understood. He wanted her so bad but he knew it was too soon. However long it might be, it would be worth the wait.

Instead of proceeding where he left off, he just put his arms around her and laid her on the bed. They lay with their arms around each other for a while. He gently rubbed her back and her stomach, trying to avoid any area that might stoke his desire. He just wanted to touch her, and she let him.

She glanced at the clock by her bed and saw it was almost dive-thirty. "Clay, we only have an hour. I need to get dressed and then we need to go." Clay hated to get up, but he did.

"Leela, can I come back after dinner?" Leela didn't know how to answer the question. She didn't have time to tell him about the condition now so maybe later would be best.

"We'll see, Clay." Then she got up. Forty-five minutes later Clay and Leela walked into the restaurant. Leela remembered being there just three days earlier on her and Clay's first date. As they stood there waiting to be seated Alex walked in the door with a very beautiful young woman.

"Laura?" Clay said. Apparently he knew her and Leela wondered how, but then it hit her. Of course he would know her - they're both from here and grew up here.

"Clay, hello, how are you?" Clay explained that he had an older sister, and she and Laura were best friends.

Alex seemed pleased that Leela had brought Clay, and she knew when he whispered to Laura as the waiter brought them to their table that he must be asking her if Clay was a good guy. Apparently she said yes, because Alex and Clay seemed to hit it off from the beginning.

Dinner was going well. Leela had liked Laura from the beginning and, Alex did seem very happy. Before dinner was over Leela felt like she had known Laura all her life, and was enjoying that feeling. As much as she enjoyed Laura she couldn't get her condition off her mind, or how the news of it would affect the two men at the table. It tore her up to think about hurting either of them. Leela became lost in those thoughts, and didn't realize that Laura was talking to her.

"What do you think?" she was asking. Leela felt so rude.

"I'm sorry, Laura, I didn't hear you. What did you ask?"

Laura smiled. She could tell something was bothering Leela at that moment, but she assumed it must be seeing her brother again after so many years - along with a soon to be sister-in-law.

"I'm thinking about having the reception at the Sailor's Club Ballroom. What do you think?" Leela smiled.

"Honestly, Laura, I don't get out much and I have never been there. I did hear some couple who came to the diner talk about their reception there, and they loved it."

Laura smiled. "I think it would be the best place. It's a lovely place, and should be just big enough for the reception."

"Leela," Alex suddenly said, "Laura and her mom are going shopping for flowers and stuff for the wedding tomorrow and I really don't want to tag along. I thought maybe we could take some more time to catch up?" Then he realized that she might have had plans with Clay. "But if you guys already have plans, that is okay, too."

Clay looked at Leela and smiled. "Actually, I have to do some work tomorrow." He knew that she needed the time with her brother.

"Sure, Alex, I'm free." Then she laughed. "My social schedule isn't all that full." She meant it to be funny, but it hurt Alex. He was blaming himself for Leela's withdrawal from life. Leela read the tension on her brother's face as she asked, "Al, what time and where?"

Laura saw they were struggling. "Well, I am meeting mom at noon so why don't you come to the hotel, Leela? They have a great little cafe there and you two can have lunch." Leela smiled at Laura. She saved the day.

"Alex smiled at his fiancée as she asked, "Is that okay with you, honey?" He loved her so much and couldn't wait to marry her, and was even enjoying the thought of having kids.

"That's okay with me. Okay, Leela?" Then they agreed.

Saying good-bye after dinner was a big deal. They all hugged like they'd never see each other again and as Clay opened the passenger side door for Leela he leaned down and kissed her forehead. It was then that he noticed she felt a bit hot.

"Are you feeling okay?" he asked after he had gotten into the car. Leela was confused, they had just had a lovely evening.

"Yeah, why?" she asked.

"You just felt a little warm," he said, and then he went on talking about Laura. Leela was shocked he had noticed she was warm, and that reminded her once again that she had to tell him. She decided she would tell Alex tomorrow at lunch, and Clay after that.

If she was getting a fever now, that meant would probably get weak and pass out soon. She needed to get rid of Clay right away because she couldn't let him see her like that, so when they got to her apartment she exaggerated a yawn.

"Clay, I'm really tired. I think I am going to go hit the sack."

He looked at her with concern. "Are you okay?"

Alex's remark about a fever had concerned Clay, and he told her so. She knew that it wasn't going to be easy to get rid of him, and if he stayed he would see the whole episode. She didn't want that.

"Clay." She began, but didn't get any further because she felt her knees starting to shake. He wasn't quite sure what was going on but he knew something was wrong. She quickly unlocked her door and pushed it open. She was running out of time, she knew the weakness would be on her in moments.

"Come in if you want, but I am horribly tired, and need to lay down." He didn't quite understand why she was rushing off to bed, but he instinctively knew something was wrong. Leela made it to the bed just in time, barely crawling under the sheets before the episode finally took her. Clay gently slid onto the bed and lay down beside her, reaching out to caress her back. As she lay there feeling him gently kneed her back with strong hands, she passed out.

Chapter 8

Saturday morning she woke up and Clay was sleeping in bed next to her with his arm around her waist. She was hoping he hadn't noticed that she passed out last night instead of just falling asleep. He had taken his clothes off and laid them neatly on the chair next to the door and was sleeping next to her with his boxers on. *He's tidy*, she mentally noted. She also noted how sexy he looked, and if she weren't sick she might have advanced the relationship, but until she came clean it was at a halt.

As she climbed out of bed she heard him turn over, just as she realized she was wearing only a tee shirt and her panties.

"Man you look good!" he said, half asleep. It was 7:30 and all Clay wanted to do was spend the day in bed with her.

"Good morning!" she said. "What time do you have to go to work?"

He smiled. "I'll go when you meet your brother. I'll drive you if you want."

She smiled. He was so nice. "I'd like that." She stood in the doorway looking at him lay there. He smiled up at her and held out his arms - they were begging for her. She slowly walked toward him, not really sure what would happen. When she reached the bed he grabbed her and threw her on the other side of the bed and started tickling her stomach. She was laughing so hard that she felt like a kid again. After a moment of wrestling around the bed he stopped and just held her. She didn't know if he moved first or if she did, all she knew was that for the first time in her life she was going to follow her heart and go where it took her.

Before she knew it he was leaning over her, kissing her like she had never been kissed before. This kiss had a destination. He then moved down her face and softly kissed her chin, then her nose. Before she knew it he had kissed every inch of her face and was moving down her neck. As she lay there she felt her knees go weak and this time it wasn't because of the condition, it was her body telling her she was ready. Her body was aching for his touch and before she knew it she had leaned up and pushed him down, climbing on top of him, straddling him, kissing his mouth, then his chin, but instead of continuing on his face she moved down.

She kissed his neck and his ear, then his bare chest. Her hands were hungry as they moved over every inch of Clay's body, and when she found what she was looking for she felt him hard and pulsating. He sat up and peeled off her tee shirt and her panties as she pulled down his boxers. She had never been in this situation but she performed as a pro as she took him in her hands and started to stroke him. Within minutes they found themselves emerging as one. It seemed like forever before they were able to catch their breath, laying side-by-side holding hands. Both satisfied like they had never been before.

Clay just lay there smiling as it hit him. *Oh my god*, he thought to himself. *That was her first time.* At that very moment she was thinking the exact same thing. Clay looked at the clock and it was almost nine o'clock. He turned to Leela and kissed her forehead.

"Are you okay, butterfly?" he asked. She smiled back at him.

"Honestly," she said, "yes." He put his arms around her and hugged her for quite some time.

"I hope I didn't hurt you," he said quietly. And she knew what he meant. She knew he was aware that it was her first.

"Clay," she answered. "It couldn't have been better." Then she pulled away and kissed his forehead.

By ten-thirty they had showered together and were now sitting on the couch watching TV. They clung to each other like it was all a dream and they didn't want to wake up. As they cuddled and laughed the phone rang.

"Hello?" Leela answered.

"Leela, how did last night go? I saw Clay picked you up from work. Did you tell him?" Leela smiled at Clay.

"Hi, Ashley. Yeah, Clay did go to dinner with me last night and he's here now, so can I call you later?" Ashley was laughing.

"You dirty dog you! Did you sleep with him?" Leela was laughing by now and Ashley could tell something had happened. Maybe she told him and everything was fine now. "Call me later, Lee," Ashley said and then she hung up. Leela quickly hung up the phone and ran back to Clay.

At eleven-thirty, Clay and Leela got into the car and he drove her to the hotel.

"Leela, you have my cell number, call me when you are ready to go. I'll come get you. I don't want you walking, okay?" She smiled at him. She was falling in love with him but she couldn't tell him. Not yet.

"Sure," she said. Then she kissed him and got out of the car.

As Leela walked into the hotel, she saw the cafe off to the right. She walked in and immediately saw Alex sitting at a table in the back with fresh sunflowers on it. The tablecloth matched with blue and white checks and sunflowers on it. It was a nice cozy little cafe. There were not a lot of people so it was a good place to talk.

When Alex saw Leela he stood up to make sure she knew where he was. As she approached the table she could see he looked a little nervous. Honestly, she was, too. It had been so long.

"Hey, Lee." Leela smiled at him.

"Hi, Alex. Thanks for asking us to dinner last night. I really enjoyed meeting Laura. She is really great." Alex smiled.

"Leela, I feel so guilty. I am so sorry for abandoning you. That is all I can think about lately." Leela was surprised, that wasn't what she was expecting.

"Alex, I'm fine. And I've been fine. You have nothing to feel guilty about." Alex wasn't convinced she was fine. There were times at dinner the previous night where she looked like a cloud hung over her.

He wasn't the only one who noticed it, Laura had mentioned it as well. They had made small talk for the first fifteen minutes as they waited for their sandwiches to arrive. When they finally did arrive, they ate in silence. Leela was nervous, she needed to tell Alex about the condition but didn't know how. His telling her how horrible he felt about keeping his distance wasn't helping. As he took his last bite he looked her in the eyes.

"Okay, Leela," he said with authority. "I may have not seen you in the last six years but I did spend every day the previous twenty years before that with you. I know that look in your eyes says you want to say something - and can't."

Leela looked down at her empty place. He could still see through her.

"Alex," she said softly. "I'm sick." Alex shook his head and looked very confused.

"What?" he asked. "Can you be a bit more specific?" She didn't really know how to explain it since she refused to read the material that the doctor gave her, so she just handed him a pamphlet from her living room. She had hidden them when Clay had gone to the bathroom and stuck one in her purse for this reason. As Alex looked at the cover he looked horrified.

"Are you sure?" he asked. "How?" She felt the tears well up in her eyes. "Let's go somewhere else," he said and he paid the check.

He walked Leela up to his and Laura's room without saying a word. He was in shock. Was she serious? As soon as they sat down at the small table by their bed he asked.

"When did you find out?"

Leela couldn't look him in the eye. "Two months ago," she said.

"How serious?" he asked.

She felt her face get flush as she said, "I don't know."

Alex stood up suddenly. "What do you mean you don't know? Didn't they tell you? Leela, this isn't something to joke about!" Leela started to cry.

"They tried to tell me and I wouldn't let them. I don't even know half the symptoms. They did put me on some medicine. They said I am considered stable now but that could change at any moment. I have blood taken once a week to monitor it."

Alex felt like he had just been gut punched. "What do you mean you don't know half the symptoms?"

Leela, still crying, answered, "I have been in denial, I guess. I refused to read the pamphlets. I guess I didn't want to know how I was going to die."

Alex got angry as he stood up. "Didn't want to know? What kind of shit is that, Leela? You need to know that to take care of yourself better. This shit is deadly!"

Leela felt anger swell up in her chest. She stood up, too, and as she did her chair flew backward. "Listen, Alex. I didn't want to know, because quite frankly, I didn't care. I had no family, no friends and a dead end job. I went to work and then came home. As far as I was concerned I could die and wouldn't have cared. Nor did I think it would affect anyone else."

That came as a slap in the face to Alex. Only she was right, she had no one. He immediately calmed down and came around to put his arms around her. She sobbed in his arms.

"You have Clay, don't you?" he asked after a few minutes. Leela wiped her eyes with a napkin that was on the table.

"I just met him earlier this week," she said in a soft voice. Alex had known that but when he saw them together he had forgotten, they seemed to have been together forever.

"I'm sorry again," Alex said to her. He had never felt as guilty in his whole life as he did at that moment. Because he left his sister six years ago she almost let herself die. And if she had died, it would have been all his fault. Then he thought of something.

"Does he know?" Leela looked up, shocked.

"No. I've tried to tell him but it never works out."

Alex took her hand. "Leela, he has a right to know." Leela nodded. She knew that.

"I shouldn't be with him," she said. Leela hadn't realized she said it out loud until she noticed the puzzled look on Alex's face.

"Why not, sis?"

Leela started to cry again. "Because I don't want to hurt him." Alex understood, but he wanted her to be happy and he saw how happy she was with him.

"Leela, you deserve to be happy. You could have a long life ahead of you. Don't sell yourself short."

After they got past the condition and all the discussions that followed, they actually had an enjoyable afternoon. They went out and Leela showed him some of the small shops along Main Street. They were sitting on a bench outside the hotel when Laura pulled up in a cab. Alex walked over to her and after paying the cab, gave her a long, passionate kiss. You could tell they were in love. She was chatting excitedly about all the things she had found for the wedding when she saw Leela sitting on the bench.

"Hey, how is it going?" She hadn't realized she was still there. It was almost five in the afternoon and Leela was expecting Clay to pick her up soon.

"Hi, Laura. Did you find a lot?" Laura smiled as she rattled off all she found. She liked Laura, and she was glad because she wanted her brother to be happy.

Leela lay in bed that night again with Clay, she had asked him to stay this time. She decided not to tell him quite yet, though, because she had enough of that for one day with Alex. They made love for a time and then just held each other. Clay sensed something was wrong but would never in a million years guess. For the second night in a row, she passed out due to the condition, next to Clay.

Chapter 9

Sunday was the last day of Alex and Laura's visit. They were leaving that evening to go back to Virginia. They had spent the morning with Laura's parents but decided to spend the afternoon with Leela and Clay. They all had fun as a group. Laura told stories about Clay as a child and Clay told stories just as embarrassing about her in return.

Then Alex and Leela went back and forth with wild stories. When it was time to go they were all disappointed.

"Ya know," Laura said, "we'll have to come back quite a bit to get things set up for the wedding. It's going to be in three and a half months and it's going to be here." Leela was happy to hear she was going to have her brother back. Then Laura turned to Leela. "I was hoping you would agree to be a bridesmaid in the wedding." Leela looked over at Alex who was beaming.

"I would love to!" she answered as she hugged her future sister-in- law.

When it was time to go and Leela was hugging her brother, he whispered in her ear, "Tell him, you'll feel better." And then they were off.

That evening Clay ordered pizza. Leela hadn't asked him to stay yet but she had assumed he was going to. It was about eight o'clock when he finally stood up.

"Well, babe, I guess I better get home." Leela stood up with a puzzled look on her face.

"You're leaving me?" she asked like a child. Clay laughed.

"Leela, I have to work early and I have to be on time.

If you tempt me with your bodily powers I may not go to sleep and I may not go to work." Leela smiled. She was going to miss sleeping near him. He sensed she felt that way.

"I'll come by for lunch tomorrow. How does that sound?" Leela nodded, not really happy with the situation but agreeing.

"Goodbye, Clay," she said. The way she said it made Clay feel like it was goodbye forever.

"Are you okay?" he asked again. He found himself asking that quite often lately, but for someone whom he had only really known for a week it seemed silly. He felt like there was something but she never budged. After he kissed her goodnight and left, she locked the door. Not long after that she felt the nightly dizziness coming on, so she crawled into bed and waited for the darkness.

Leela climbed out of bed early on Monday morning. She had to make her weekly visit to the clinic to see the vampires and she had forgotten about that when she begged Clay to stay the previous night. As soon as she remembered she was thankful he went home. It would have been hard to tell him why she was leaving early without telling him where she was going.

It was five-thirty and Leela wanted to be at the clinic by six forty-five so she could get to work on time. Leela put her work cloths on and grabbed her apron. By six twenty-five she was making the fifteen-minute walk.

Thankfully the clinic wasn't busy, when Leela walked through the door there was only a handful of people there. She signed in at the registration desk and was seated by a table with a couple of magazines on it. As she picked up the top magazine the woman behind the desk called her name.

"Leela Jacobs, come on back." Leela put the magazine down and walked back through the door. Leela knew the drill. She sat down, pulled her sleeve up, verified her address and phone number and let them stick her.

Sometimes the vampire would make small talk but Leela never really responded. It generally only took them about five minutes to finish.

"Okay, Leela," the lady said. "Dr. Risinger wanted me to ask you just a few questions, to go along with the results of this draw."

Leela nodded her head. "Okay, dear, do you feel any weakness of the legs or knees?" Leela nodded once again. "And how often?"

Leela sighed. "It depends. Mostly before bed - but every once in a while during the day, too. Anywhere from one to three times a day." The vampire nodded.

"Any blackouts?"

Leela sighed. "Yes, right after the weakened knees." The vampire nodded again.

"Any coughing of blood?"

Leela shook her head. "No, none."

The vampire got up. "Okay, Leela, you're free to go. I suppose that Dr. Risinger will want to see you this week - if you start coughing blood call him immediately." Leela thanked her and left the clinic.

Great she thought. *I'm going to cough blood next.*

Leela actually arrived at work earlier than normal. When she walked in about seven- thirty Sammy was sitting at the counter counting the money for the register. "Hey, Leela, early today?" Sammy had been in the best mood since she found out she was pregnant.

"Yeah," she answered back. Sammy was giving Leela a sly smile. "So what is going on with the hunk from last week?" Leela smiled. "We spent the weekend together. He is great." Sammy was beaming. In the seven weeks she knew Leela she never smiled like that. She was so happy for Leela.

"Leela, I wanted to talk to you about your doctor's appointments." Leela froze. "I know that you go see a doctor pretty often, more than normal. Is something wrong?" Leela's smile disappeared.

"Actually, Sammy, I've just been feeling more tired lately and the doctors are just running tests to make sure nothing's wrong." She lied. She was afraid to lose her job. Sammy seemed satisfied

"Okay, keep me posted."

By eight o'clock Leela and two other waitress were waiting tables, and it was discount day again. Leela was concerned because Ashley wasn't at work yet. She asked Sammy if she had heard from her and she shook her head no. Leela was really beginning to worry now, this wasn't like Ashley.

At quarter after eight she decided to call her. As she picked up the phone to dial the bell on the front door chimed and it was Ashley coming through it.

"I was worried," Leela said as she put the phone down.

As Ashley rushed to put on her apron on she explained, "Ryan was sick this morning and couldn't go to school. I couldn't find a sitter so I had to take a cab and take him to his grandma's across town. I'm sorry. I should have called. Is Sammy mad?" Leela let out a loud breath. She had been worried and she was just relieved that Ashley was okay.

"No, she was worried, too. She's in her office."

While Ashley went to tell Sammy her story Leela went out to serve tables.

The diner was busy and she didn't even notice when Clay walked through the door and sat at the counter a little after eleven. She was waiting on her last table before her lunch break when she saw him sitting at the counter having a conversation with Ashley. As she approached, he turned to her and kissed her on the cheek and Leela blushed.

"Hi, beautiful!" he said happily. Leela smiled back. She had missed him since he left the night before. Ashley could tell they were happy with each other and decided to leave them alone.

"Can you get out of here for a while?" Leela wanted so

badly to kiss him but didn't want to do it in the diner.

"I have half an hour for lunch." With a grin he grabbed her hand and pulled her out onto the busy sidewalk. As soon as they were away from the diner he stopped and pulled her close. She felt his hand touch her chin and tip her head up so he could look her in her eyes.

When she thought she couldn't wait any longer he kissed her - a long, passionate kiss. When he pulled away, she felt her knees go weak. This time it wasn't the condition; it was a good kind of weakness. He pulled her into his car. As she got in, she saw there was two sandwiches wrapped up sitting in the middle of his seat.

"I brought lunch," he said as he handed her one. They sat in his car and ate. Then they talked about the weekend. "Leela?" he asked hesitantly. Leela stopped eating and looked at him. She sensed something was wrong.

"Clay, what's wrong?" He didn't know how to quite put this without upsetting her. They were just getting to know each other and he was afraid she would regress and decide she didn't want to see him. After all, they had only been seeing each other a week.

"Leela, my job is sending me on a project out of town." Leela felt her heart stop.

"For how long?" Clay didn't really know.

"I don't know, Leela. I just found out today. I don't leave for a week. But it could last months." Leela was having trouble breathing. She let him in and now he was leaving her.

"Clay? Where are you going?" Not that it mattered.

"D.C. I am going to be programming some computers for a communication company. It's not all that far away. I can come home on weekends." Leela tried to hold them back, but tears welled up in her eyes.

"Please, Leela, this doesn't mean we can't be together. It's just an obstacle. We'll work around this." Leela couldn't help it. She was so upset, and at that particular moment she couldn't see how it would work. Leela saw the clock on his car radio and it was time for her to go back to work.

"I have to go," she said and he tried to stop her, but she just got out of the car and ran back into the diner. Ashley saw Leela crying when she walked into the diner.

"Oh, honey! What's wrong?" Leela looked at Ashley.

"His job is sending him away for the next few months. He is going to Washington D.C." Ashley saw that Leela was crushed.

"Leela, what did he say?" Leela shook her head.

"He said it wouldn't change anything and that he'd come home on weekends and we could still be together. I just don't believe it." Ashley knew how hard it was for Leela to let Clay get close to her. Everyone Leela had ever loved left her in one way or another.

"Lee, baby, you have to give him a chance." Ashley knew that she hadn't told Clay about the condition yet and now she doubted Leela ever would.

The last half of the day went by quickly and Leela was busy waiting tables. At the end of their shift Ashley asked Leela if she could walk home with her. Since they lived two blocks apart the walk was the same way for the most part. Leela said "Sure," but she really didn't feel like talking.

She had to make a decision. Would she continue to see Clay even though he was leaving? Ashley tried to tell her to calm down and told her not read so much into it, but Leela couldn't help it. She was convinced this was a sign for her to stop. She had no right consuming Clay's life when she had this condition that could take her away any day. She expressed these feelings to Ashley. Ashley felt sorry for her because she knew it wasn't true, but she couldn't tell Leela that. When it came time for Leela to go her own way Ashley gave her a hug.

"I'm here for you, honey. I have to go get Ryan but I'll be home in an hour if you want to call or come by. And give him a chance - you deserve it." Then they walked their separate ways.

Chapter 10

Leela walked through her door and locked it behind her; she wasn't going to let anyone in. The first thing she noticed after locking the door was the light on the answering machine blinking.

"*Message one*...Leela, it's Al. Thought I'd call and let you know that we got home okay and that I enjoyed our time together. Call me sometime."

Leela thought maybe she'd call her brother. At one time she could have talked to him about something like this.

"*Message two*...Leela, it's Clay. I'm sorry I upset you earlier but I can't help it. My job requires it. Like I said, this doesn't have to end. I truly believe I am falling in love with you so please don't push me away. I promise to come home every weekend and we can talk throughout the week. Please, Leela, call me back."

As she listened to the message from Clay she started to cry again.

"*Message three*...This message is for Leela Jacobs. This is Paulina, the nurse at Dr. Risinger's office. We have the results of your blood test this morning and want you to come in tomorrow at two for an appointment. This is important so we hope you can make it, but if the time won't work, please call us back." The nurse left a number.

She was getting worse. She knew she was, otherwise Dr. Risinger wouldn't want to see her. It was another sign. *Don't ruin Clay's life*, she thought. As her answering machine went off her phone started to ring. She knew it was probably Clay and she didn't have the strength to talk to him, so she let the machine pick it up.

"Leela? I know you're home. Please pick up! I need to talk to you, baby. Things will be okay. I promise." Leela so desperately wanted to believe him but she knew what she had to do. At that moment she made up her mind. Instead of listening to the rest of what Clay had to say she turned the machine off.

Leela didn't feel very hungry so she didn't eat any dinner that night. The phone had rung five times and she knew it had to be Clay. She decided to call Alex. "Hello?" She heard Laura's voice.

"Hi, Laura, is Alex around?"

"Oh, Hi, Leela. He's right here, hold on." A second later he was on the phone.

"Hey, Leela," Alex said cheerfully. Leela didn't know what to say, she had been upset and crying all evening and here he was in a good mood. She didn't want to ruin it so she decided not to keep her problems to herself. They talked about his trip home and their weekend.

As Leela decided it was time to hang up Alex asked, "Leela, what's wrong?" He could always tell when something was bothering her. Before she knew what she was doing, she had let it all out. Everything from Clay's moving to her doctor's appointment. Alex told her to give Clay a chance, if he said it would be all right then it would be. He agreed with Ashley that she was foolish to think all of this was a sign for her to let him go. By the time they did hang up an hour later she still didn't feel any better. They didn't know what it was like to be her. They couldn't. They were all living a healthy life.

The phone had rung several more times that night. Leela felt tears swell up in her chest every time. Why couldn't her life be normal? For years Leela had been an unnoticeable person to the world. Now she wished she still was. It was getting late and she decided she might as well go to bed. When she got up, her legs gave out and she felt dizzy, and as she fell to the floor she tried to catch herself and hit her head on the coffee table. Half an hour later Leela awoke on the floor to the sound of pounding at her door, she had been knocked unconscious by the fall.

She was too weak to answer the door so she just lay there. It was then that she noticed the puddle of blood soaking into the carpet where her head had been. She reached up and touched her forehead and felt a big gash, and it was still bleeding.

Ashley stood outside Leela's door banging on it. She was worried about her. She had called several times and didn't get an answer. Ryan was at a neighbor's so she decided to come over and make sure she was okay. Ashley yelled, "Leela, honey, are you okay?" Leela heard Ashley's voice outside and desperately wanted to let her in but couldn't get up. So she dragged herself to the door and reached up and unlocked it. Ashley heard it and opened the door.

"Oh my god!" she said as she saw Leela lying on the floor bleeding. "I'm calling for an ambulance." Leela panicked.

"No, please don't. I'm fine. This is a side effect." Ashley knew what she was talking about but she had a deep cut on her head that looked like it needed attention. Ashley saw that Leela wouldn't let her call and ambulance.

"Okay," she said, giving in. "Let me take you to the emergency room then and get cut stitched up." Leela had seen all the blood and decided that it might be a good idea to go. Ashley called for a cab and helped Leela up off the floor.

The emergency room was nearly empty when they got there so Leela had her head looked at almost immediately. Leela made Ashley promise not to tell them how she did it, and told her that she would see her doctor tomorrow so it would be okay. With a bit of trepidation Ashley agreed to keep quiet about Leela's illness. It took an hour for them to complete everything and by eleven they were on their way home.

Ashley talked Leela into not going to work the next day, Sammy would understand because Ashley was going to make her understand. Leela promised to call Ashley after her appointment, and Ashley promised not to say anything to Clay if he came into the diner.

The next day when Leela woke up she called Sammy and explained her situation. She didn't want Sammy to know that she had lied so Leela simply said her doctor had called and wanted to see her after her late night emergency room visit. Sammy understood and told her she could have the day off. Leela volunteered for a shift on Saturday to make up the time and Sammy agreed.

Leela took her time getting up and moving, and had barely gotten herself dressed when she heard a knock at her door around noon. She ran out of her room to the living room and looked out the peephole and found clay standing on her front stoop. She didn't want to answer his knock. *He must have already gone by the diner or he wouldn't have known I'm home.*

"Baby, are you here?" Leela heard the panic in his voice. She wondered what Ashley had told him, even though she promised not to say anything. "Leela, I'm worried. Please answer." She felt weak and she missed him. If it hadn't happened to her, she would have thought it absurd to think someone could fall in love after only a week. And yet here she was, missing him too much not to let him in.

Leela slowly opened the door with plans to tell him she hit her head and had a routine check-up today. A look of horror crossed his face as he saw the big bandage on her forehead.

"Oh, baby, what happened?" he asked as he walked in and took her hands in his. Leela immediately started to cry. She couldn't help it, she wanted him to never leave her and he was. Maybe it would work if she was healthy, but she wasn't.

"I tripped last night over my shoes and hit my head on the table. I got stitches." She was so dramatic that he cringed.

"I'm so sorry, baby. Can we talk for a minute? I have to get back to work soon." She was glad to hear he didn't plan on staying.

"Leela, I went to work today and told my boss I couldn't go to D.C." She was shocked and amazed, she hadn't expected him to do that. "He said he could reassign it but it would take two weeks to do. So I would have to start the job next week and then let someone else take over." He put his arms around her. "I would do anything to be with you, and that includes quitting my job. Would you be okay with me starting this project? I would only spend two weeks away - and I promise to be back on the weekends." She was in shock and didn't know what to say. She should have been happy but she wasn't. Clay making this sacrifice for her meant she would have to tell him her secret, and soon.

"Leela, honey, say something." He was begging her with a dumbfounded look. She smiled at him, not knowing yet what to say.

"Can you come back after work?" She wanted to be with him, and that meant telling him. He smiled, and was both glad and relieved that she was inviting him back.

"I get off at four-thirty. I'll be here by five." She kissed him and he held her for a long moment before reluctantly pulling away. All of Leela's tears had dried by the time Clay had walked to his car, and she felt like her broken heart had been mended.

At two o'clock Leela was called into Dr. Risinger's office by his nurse, Paulina. Leela sat on an exam table in a gown while Paulina took her blood pressure and pulse, both of which were below normal. She asked her several questions about her condition before asking about the big bandage on her forehead.

Leela told Paulina about her legs going weak and the

blackout that caused her fall. The nurse asked her if she had been coughing up any blood and Leela shook her head no. Paulina left the room and told her that Dr. Risinger would be in shortly, and two minutes later the doctor walked into the room.

"Good afternoon, Leela, how are you today?" Leela wasn't quite sure what kind of answer he wanted.

"I'm hanging in there, Doctor," she answered.

"Paulina told me about your fall last night. It must have been scary." Leela again didn't know what to say so this time she said nothing. "Leela, for the last month we have been monitoring your blood gas levels. So far they have held steady, but this last draw showed a change." Leela felt panic rise in her chest. "Your levels have dropped and that's not a good thing. Your condition has three stages. You were at stage one and the drop is a sign that you may have moved to stage two. I can confirm that with a few more simple tests. With stage two comes new symptoms. You will still get the weakness and the blacking out after a strenuous day. It may happen more often - in the middle of a day - and maybe for no reason at all. You may start coughing up blood. Doesn't sound pleasant and it isn't. This is becoming serious, and you will need new medication to keep you at stage two. Stage three almost always requires hospitalization for continual care. You do not want to reach stage three, so it's crucial that we get this under control." The doctor could see tears in Leela's eyes.

"You don't have to die, Leela. If you take care of yourself you could live a long, happy life. The medication can control it." The doctor left the room to put in the order for the tests and Leela couldn't hold it back any longer. The tears began to flow as she thought of Clay.

There was no way she could drag him into this. He deserved to love someone who would give him a long, happy life. She was sure that she couldn't. Leela didn't have the strength to deal with this herself and there was no way she could give anyone else strength. He would want children, and that would put Leela at serious risk. Her mind was clouded with thoughts of Clay when the doctor came back in.

Two hours later Leela walked down Main Street in the rain. It was four o'clock and Clay would be getting home from work soon. She wasn't up to telling him; emotional strain always took her strength away. She reached her street and as she turned down it she saw Clay's car. It was parked in front of her place and he was sitting on the steps, drenched from the downpour.

"You're early," she said to him as he stood up.

"Leela, are you okay?" He knew where she had been. Ashley had to have told him, and she was furious.

"What do you mean?" She snapped. He took a step back.

"I've been calling you for the last 3 hours and I went by the diner and Sammy told me you were at the doctor. My sister called me and apparently Laura told her that you weren't okay. Is that true?"

Her face turned red as the rain dripped from her hair.

"I'm fine, okay! I went to the doctor because I have a big fat cut on my head, Clay." She was angry for being so stupid. Of course Alex would tell Laura, and Clay's sister was Laura's best friend. She should have realized it would get around. He apparently didn't know all the details because his face instantly softened.

"Leela, I was just worried." She, too, let it go and they stood in the rain holding each other.

Leela returned to work on Wednesday and things went back to normal from there. Clay spent the nights with her after work and stayed most nights. He was leaving town on Sunday and she dreaded it. Her brother had called and she had given him a hard time about Laura's slip and he promised that it wouldn't happen again. Then Laura apologized herself, saying she hadn't realized Clay didn't know. He didn't, and every time Leela tried to tell him she couldn't. She knew that he deserved to know but she just couldn't.

Friday evening Leela and Clay went to Ashley's house for dinner. This was the first time they were going to meet Ryan. He was a happy boy and so smart, he could carry on a conversion with an adult for hours and never be lost. Leela was impressed by him and told Ashley so when they had a minute alone.

Ryan had dragged Clay into his room to play trucks and the girls were cleaning the kitchen. Ashley knew all about Leela's doctor's appointment and worried about her constantly.

"He is good with kids," Ashley commented. She hadn't realized that the condition would prevent Leela from having a normal pregnancy. If she had then she never would have said what she said next.

"Leela, you should marry him and have lots of kids. You both are good with them." Leela didn't answer. She tried not to look at her friend because there were tears in her eyes. By the time Ashley realized what she had done it was too late.

"Oh, Lee, I'm sorry. I didn't think." Leela was quick to reassure Ashley that she was okay, but really she wasn't. Leela was feeling optimistic because she hadn't had a dizzy spell in two days and thought maybe the tests were wrong. It was wishful thinking but she knew it wasn't true.

After the kitchen was clean, Ashley put Ryan to bed and the three of them sat in the living room with a bottle of wine and talked. Leela was enjoying herself but it was getting late and Clay would be leaving in two days. She wanted to try to tell him before he left. She hoped she could.

It was almost ten o'clock when they walked in her front door. Clay immediately turned his attention to her, urging her towards the bedroom. He playfully threw her into the bed and quickly followed after her. She had really wanted to tell him, and even hesitated for a moment before giving in to his tender touch. As they were making love he whispered in her ear that he wanted her to have his children. She tensed for a moment at his words, giving clay pause.

She did not plan on telling him while they were making love, but his words played over and over again in her mind. Even though he asked what was wrong and she said nothing, Clay knew better. That night as they lay in bed he held her tight, held her as if she would disappear if he let her go.

"You don't want kids?" he finally asked her. He couldn't get her reaction to his words out of his head. After spending all evening with Ryan, he had thought about it. He hadn't meant to say it, it had just slipped out in a moment of passion.

Leela was tired and afraid that the darkness would come soon. "Clay, it's only been two weeks. Don't you think it's a bit soon to be thinking about kids?" She tried to make it sound humorous, but he sensed that she meant something else.

"Leela, I have fallen in love with you. I would hope you love me, too. In the last two weeks I realized you are the one I want to spend my life with. I want to grow old with you." Those words made Leela tear up. She would never be old, but she couldn't tell him that now.

All she said was, "Clay, I do love you." Then darkness set in.

Chapter 11

It was Monday morning and Leela was on her way to work. She had just left the clinic and her weekly visit to the vampires. Clay had left the night before and she already missed him so much. She felt guilty, though, because she hadn't told him. As she got onto Main Street she saw Ashley running to catch up to her.

"Hey, Lee!" Ashley hadn't called her all weekend because she knew that she needed the time with Clay. As soon as she looked at Leela she knew she hadn't told him. Leela had this look of disappointment in her eyes.

"I couldn't do it!" she cried.

"It's okay, you will," but Ashley wasn't sure she ever would.

The week was uneventful, and when Clay called every night they talked for hours at a time. He was looking forward to coming home on Friday night to see her. She was too, but she had also decided that it was time - no more stalling. On Saturday she was going to sit him down and tell him. She told him on Thursday that she had something very important to tell him, and that he should not let her forget. She figured that way he would make her tell him.

Her brother had called twice that week to check on her. She had updated him on her condition and made him promise to tell Laura not to tell Clay's sister. Alex was upset with her for not telling Clay.

"He has a right to know!" he said more than once. Leela knew Alex was right and told him that she planned on doing it on the coming weekend. Alex was so worried about her and didn't think she was taking her condition seriously enough. She told him he worried too much, but he didn't care, he wanted to be in every part of her life now. He had spent the last six years without his sister, and he was determined to make up for it.

On Friday she started having a coughing fit as she sat on her front porch waiting for Clay, and when she finished she found blood all over the porch. She was horrified. She had thought she was doing well, but now the symptoms were getting worse. She was officially in stage two. She panicked, Clay was going to be there any minute and he couldn't see the blood. She ran inside and got a big glass of water and dumped it on the porch. It didn't clear it all up so she ran inside and grabbed another one.

As she got back to the porch with glass in hand her knees went weak and she fell. This time as she blacked out, she didn't just hit a table, she fell down the concrete steps onto the walk.

Clay was walking down the sidewalk when he saw Leela on her porch, and was puzzled when he saw her pouring water out onto the concrete. As he got closer he saw her collapse and tumble down the stairs. He ran the short distance to her and found her unconscious with dark blood staining her shirt. When he saw the pooled blood Leela had been trying to wash away on the porch, he panicked.

"Leela, baby! Wake up!" He was shaking her but she wasn't moving. He pulled his cell phone out of his pocket and dialed 911.

When Leela came to, she had several paramedics around her and she was strapped down to a hard board. She hurt all over and had a moment of panic before she remembered she had blacked out and fallen down the stairs. Her head had been immobilized so her view was limited, but she could see Clay hovering directly behind the ambulance personnel. He had a frightened look on his face. He had thought she was dead, It scared him so much his eyes were full of tears. A look of relief crossed his face when he realized she was conscious and looking at him.

"Baby, what happened?" She knew that the paramedics who were working on her would need to know about her condition.

"I'm sorry," she said to him. He didn't know what she meant. Then she turned to the paramedic at her side and told him about her blood disease, and that she was in stage two. She told the paramedic about the blood-laden cough and blacking out. When she looked back up at Clay the look of confusion in his eyes pained her.

"I couldn't tell you." She started to cry.

The paramedics were trying to calm her down as she suffered some really bad cuts and bruises in the fall, and they were unsure of the extent of her injuries. Clay was confused. *What did she just say*?

"Leela, what does that mean?"

A paramedic that was standing between them took him by the arm and pulled him aside. "Sir, we need to keep her calm. Let me try and explain." Clay just stared at the paramedic in disbelief as the man told him the woman he loved would most likely die in the near future if she really was in the stage two.

Leela could see the paramedic talking to Clay and she saw the mixed look of fear and horror on his face. *They must be telling him what I have*, she thought to herself. When he looked into her eyes she could tell he knew.

The paramedics took Leela to the hospital where she went through x-rays to make sure nothing was broken. Clay stood by her side the whole time, but stayed silent. She wasn't sure what to say to him so they were both quiet.

"You're a lucky woman," the doctor said as he came into the examining room. "No broken bones and just minor cuts and bruises." The doctor was well aware of her condition and knew that the fall was caused by her blackout. "I'd take it easy if I were you, Ms. Jacobs. And it probably isn't a good idea to be alone much."

Leela didn't know what to say. She was always alone. Especially now that Clay was working out of town. "I'm going to discharge you now. Be careful and make sure to schedule a follow up with...Dr. Risinger. He is your primary doctor, right?" Leela nodded her head. It hurt, she felt like she was black and blue all over. "And I don't want you to go back to work until you feel like it. So I am going to give you an open doctor's excuse and you can fill in the date when you're ready." Leela thanked him and they walked in silence to Clay's car.

As they drove home Clay looked at her.

"How long have you known?" He meant the condition, and didn't have to say it. She knew he was going to be upset that she hadn't told him sooner. They had been together almost three weeks.

She answered his question quietly, "Almost three months." He didn't want to be mad at her with her so sick, but he couldn't help it.

"Leela, were you ever going to tell me? I thought you were dead lying there on the sidewalk." She looked down at her lap. Tears were sliding down her cheeks.

"I tried," she said. "I'm sorry," she started to sob. "You don't deserve this, you don't deserve me. You want someone that can give you lots of kids and someone you can grow old with, and, Clay, that's not me." He didn't know what to say. He had wanted all she said. But he had wanted her, too.

"You don't have to stay tonight," she said in between her sobs. Clay stopped the car on the side of the road in front of her place.

"Leela, you can't be alone. The doctor said so." She felt like he was only staying for that reason.

"I don't want you to feel like you have to babysit me. You don't want to be here. I hurt you and I'm sorry. Please, just go."

Clay was confused. He wanted to stay but she was right - he was angry with her. Three weeks and she hadn't told him. They had shared their life and she still never told him. Her sister had been right, but when he asked her about it, Leela had lied to him. She got out of the car and slowly limped her way up the stairs. He meant to get out and help her, but his legs wouldn't move. When she realized she was alone her eyes filled with tears.

He just sat in his car watching her, letting the tears flow. Leela locked the door behind her then she slid down the door to the floor and cried. She hated he had to find out like that and knew it must have been horrible for him. She had hurt him badly, so badly that he didn't want to be with her. She sat there and cried.

Clay sat in his car outside her apartment realizing he was not being very supportive of her. She hadn't told him - and she might have lied to him - but she was trying to protect his feelings, right? He was confused, he had never felt this way about a woman before. He did want her to have his children - and he did want to grow old with her - but she said it wasn't possible. The paramedic had told him that 75% of the people diagnosed with her condition die within the first year, but he doctor in the emergency room had said that if she was careful and took her medicine she could live a long and nearly normal life.

Deciding he was being a jerk, Clay bolted from the car and ran up the steps to the door.

"Leela? Baby, I'm sorry. Please open the door." Leela was lying up against the door sobbing because she knew she had hurt him. She also knew that if she continued to see him that she was going to hurt him more, and he deserved more than that.

Clay stood at the door and knocked for a long time. Leela didn't say anything as he pleaded through the locked door. "Leela," he said, "it's not your fault. You can't help it. I understand why you couldn't tell me. I was a jerk. Please, Leela, please. I love you." Then it was quiet and she knew he had left.

Clay sat in his car, afraid to leave. *What if it happened again?* She could die alone and he didn't want that, so slept in his car that night outside of her place.

Chapter 12

Leela must have fallen asleep on the floor in front of the door because she woke up hurting all over Saturday morning at just after daylight. She needed pain medicine. The doctor had given her some, but told her that it may affect the medication she was taking on a regular basis so not to take them together. As she climbed to her feet moaning in pain, she passed by the front window. She saw that Clay's car was still out front and as she looked closer she realized he was still in it. He must have slept there. Her head was pounding as she felt sadness swell up in her heart. She wanted to run out there and let him hold her, let him tell her it was going to be okay, but she couldn't.

"He deserves more," she just kept saying to herself. She picked up the phone and dialed his cell number. On the first ring he picked it up, he hadn't been sleeping.

"Leela?" He was hoping it was her, who else could it have been at five-thirty in the morning?

"Clay, go home," she said in a soft voice. "Get some sleep." He didn't want to go home, he wanted to come in.

"Leela, let me in. Please!" he was begging her. Hearing his voice and how much pain was in it hurt her horribly.

"Clay, I'm no good for you. I can't give you the things you need to be happy. I lied to you and I deceived you. You deserve more." Clay couldn't believe what he was hearing. She seemed so calm, too. He was afraid she was giving up and he wasn't ready to let her do that.

"Leela, listen. I wont be happy unless I have you. You didn't lie to me or deceive me, you were protecting me because you didn't want to hurt me. You have done nothing wrong, baby. Are you listening to me? I need you. I love you." Leela was trying hard to maintain her composure. She didn't want him to know how much she was hurting inside.

"Let me in, please." He was begging again. She could tell by the quiver in his voice that he had been crying. She had hurt him badly.

"I am so sorry I've hurt you, Clay. From the beginning I didn't want to get too close. I didn't realize I would fall in love with you so quickly. It's not fair to you to be sold short with me." Clay was getting noticeably frustrated.

"Leela, I need you. I want you. With my support you can live a long life. Please don't give up." But she already had.

"No, Clay, I can't. The reality of it is that with or without your support, I can't do it." Then she hung up. He tried to call back but she wouldn't pick up the phone, she had made up her mind.

Clay sat out in the car staring up at the apartment window that he knew was her bedroom. She had given up. She was all alone and it was his fault. If he would have just gotten up and helped her into the house he would be in there at this very moment. He was a fool. He started his car and drove home, where he made a quick phone call and stayed in bed until noon.

Leela stood in the kitchen window watching Clay drive away. She had tears running down her face. He was the best thing that had ever happened to her and it was a shame that she wasn't the best thing that had happened to him. With a heavy heart Leela made her way to the bedroom to lay down.

She was sleeping sound until she heard the phone ring at about ten o'clock. She assumed it was Clay so she didn't get up, but when she heard the answering machine pick up she realized it was Alex.

"Leela? Leela? Are you home? Pick up, I'm worried

about you. Clay called me this morning and told me about your fall. He is pretty shaken up, too, Lee. You shouldn't be so hard on him."

Leela was going to get out of bed and pick up the phone until she heard he had already talked to Clay. She knew that Alex would tell her not to shut Clay out - that he loved her and she needed him. But she had made up her mind and didn't need any criticism from Alex about it. He didn't understand - he simply couldn't. He was happy and about to marry the girl he loved, and more importantly, he wasn't sick.

"Leela, I am worried about you," he continued on the machine. "I am you brother, damn it, now pick up! You can't shut me out!" He was upset. The story Clay had told him terrified him. But as she listened to her brother's voice on the machine Leela laughed in her bed.

"I can't shut him out, huh?" she said. "Just watch me. I can do it as good as you can, Alexander Jacobs."

As if Alex had actually heard her he snapped. "That's it, Lee. I'm coming down." He hung up the phone. Leela sat up in bed so fast that her head started to spin. He isn't really coming, is he? She thought to herself.

At that same moment Alex was throwing clothes into a suitcase and explaining everything to Laura. It was Saturday morning, and he was going to drive down there and come back on Monday - if everything was okay. He told her that he was afraid to leave Leela alone. She understood and kissed him on his cheek.

"Drive safely," she said, and he left.

He was an hour away when he decided to call Clay.

"Hello?" Clay answered the phone and Alex could tell he had woken Clay up. He knew Clay spent the whole night parked in front of Leela's place worried sick.

"Clay, it's Alex. I wanted to let you know that Leela has shut me out, too."

Clay sighed. "I don't know what to do, Alex. I love her."

Alex knew that.

"I'm on my way there, Clay."

Clay sat up in bed.

"Here? Like to Palmside?" He had no idea what made Alex make the drive, but he knew it had to be serious. "Is she okay?"

"I don't know. That is why I'm coming."

Clay looked at the clock and saw it was almost noon.

"Thanks for calling," he said. "Call me when you get in. I need to know that she is okay." Alex said he would and they hung up.

Leela had called Ashley and told her about what had happened, starting with the fall and Clay finding her, and then her brother driving down. Ashley offered to come over but Leela said she wanted to be alone. Ashley wanted to tell Leela that she was being a fool and that she needed to let Clay take care of her, but she didn't. She was well aware that Leela was shutting anyone with an opinion out and she didn't want to be included.

Ashley knew that Clay would be worried sick about Leela, so she called him to let him know as of now she was okay. Clay was grateful she did, because he had been worried sick after Alex called and said she hadn't picked up the phone.

Leela was sitting on her couch watching TV when she heard a knock at the door. She assumed it was Clay again, so she didn't get up. If she looked at him through the peephole she was liable to let him in. She missed him so much.

The knocking persisted, followed by a raised voice. She couldn't place it but it wasn't Clay's.

"Leela, Leela?" Then she realized it was Alex. She could not believe he drove all the way from Virginia just because she didn't answer her phone. She got up and opened the door. Alex looked a wreck because he had been so worried about her. As he walked in, he grabbed her and hugged her. She felt how tense he was and she pulled away, he actually had tears in his eyes.

"Alex, it's okay. I'm okay." They walked over to the couch and sat down. "Alex, Clay was wrong to call and worry you. I am just as okay as I was the last time I saw you." Alex couldn't stop staring at the nasty bruises all over her face. She had forgotten about them.

"Leela, I was so worried. Why didn't you answer the phone when I called?" Leela lied.

"I was sleeping, Alex. We had a long night." Alex knew it was a lie, but he hadn't driven across two states to argue with her.

They sat and talked for the next few hours. They didn't leave the house because Leela didn't want anyone to see her bruises. Leela had told Alex to go home the next day because she didn't want him missing work and Alex said he would see. He knew that Clay had to leave for D.C. the next day and desperately wanted to talk Leela into seeing him before he left.

The next morning as Leela and Alex sat eating breakfast the phone rang. Alex was already here, so Leela knew it must be Clay calling.

"Answer it, Lee," Alex urged. Leela got up and stomped over to the phone.

"Hello," she said softly. At first Clay didn't say anything because he hadn't expected her to answer. "Hello?" she said again a bit louder.

"It's me," he said, waiting for her to hang up. After a silent moment he said, "Are you still there?"

Leela nodded and then realizing he couldn't see her nod responded. "Yes."

"I love you, baby. Please don't shut me out. I leave tonight so please, let me see you."

Leela had tears in her eyes. Alex was watching her, urging her to let him come. "Clay, I can't, I told you. I'm no good for you." Alex stood up. That wasn't what he wanted her to say. On the other end of the phone line Clay was shaking. He didn't know what to say to make her open up.

"Okay," he said to her. "You may not think you are good for me. I'll let you think that, but let me make the decision of whether or not I want you. And I do, Leela. I do." Leela stood there not sure what to say. She looked at Alex and his eyes pleaded with her.

"All right, but Alex is here." Then Clay let out a cry of relief.

"I'll be there in fifteen, I love you." Then he hung up. Alex was satisfied.

"Leela, I'm going to go out for a while but I will see you for dinner." Leela didn't really want Alex to leave.

"You don't have to go." Alex knew that he didn't have to but he wanted to. He would stay long enough for Clay to get there. Leela shook her head and before they could sit back down Clay was knocking at the door.

Alex let him in. Clay thanked him for doing whatever he did with Leela. He was sure that if Alex hadn't shown up he'd still be sitting on the front porch. Alex put on his jacket and told them both goodbye.

Clay was still standing in the doorway not really sure what to do or say. Leela was equally confused, so much had happened Friday night. It wasn't his fault and it wasn't her fault. There was an awkward silence between the two of them as they stood there.

Clay couldn't stand it any longer so he walked over to Leela and took her hand. She let him lead her to the couch where he sat down next to her and held her. Neither of them spoke as he stroked her hair. It was at that moment he knew that he couldn't live without her and was willing to accept any future he had to - as long as it was with her. It seemed like forever before she said anything to him.

"Clay, I am truly sorry I didn't tell you sooner." He just nodded. He didn't want to think about it anymore.

"Leela, I don't want to talk about the past, okay?" Leela nodded her head. "But," he said, "You have to promise me that you will tell me everything from now on." Leela nodded again. She let down her guard completely with him. She had spent the last twelve hours preparing for a life without him and now she was promised a life with him.

"Maybe this isn't the right time to ask, after all, it's only been three weeks, but I have never in my life felt like this, and I know it's right. Leela, will you marry me?" Leela looked up with surprise. She hadn't expected him to say that, especially not now. She didn't know what to say, so she didn't say anything.

"Leela, I want to take care of you. Please let me." Leela looked Clay in the eye and she could tell he meant every word he said. Marry him? It had only been a few weeks and he had just learned that she was sick. She was sure he wasn't in his right frame of mind.

"Leela, I'm serious!" he said as he looked at her with tears in his eyes.

"Clay, it's too soon. Let's not talk about this right now. Of course I love you but marriage is a big step, and you have so much going for you right now. I have so much going on right now - let's just see what unfolds in the future." He looked hurt. He had expected to have to convince her but he had expected her to eventually say yes. She could see by looking at him that he was hurt.

"Clay, I do love you. I don't want you to ask me in fear. I want you to have time to really understand my condition and then accept it if you can. I'm not even sure I can accept it, to be honest with you. It's been months and I still haven't even begun to. One month ago I was sure I would die alone. Now you're here and Alex is here. I just need time to adjust and think." He knew that she was being reasonable so he just nodded before slipping his arms tight around her waist.

Alex was coming back for dinner and then he would be heading home to Virginia. Clay would be leaving in a few hours as well, and then Leela would be all alone.

"Come with me, Leela!" Clay asked her before Alex

arrived. "It's only for a week and you shouldn't go back to work yet anyway." His eyes pleaded with her. "Please, Leela, I can't leave you again." Leela looked at him and realized how lucky she was.

"Clay, you'll be working. I'll still be alone. Anyway, I can probably go back to work in a few days." Clay shook his head.

"Leela, I'll see you in the evenings after work, and in the mornings. I can see you at lunchtime. Please. I'll be right there if anything happens." He was begging her.

"I'll think about it," she answered, knowing she didn't have much time. He was leaving in three hours.

When Alex showed up ten minutes later Leela was in the kitchen ordering Chinese delivery for dinner. When she walked into the living room Clay was telling Alex that he wanted Leela to join him for the week in D.C.

"Leela, it's a good idea. You'll have lots to do during the day. That place is great!" Leela was shaking her head, they were ganging up on her. They were the most important men in her life - actually the only men in her life - and she could tell they both loved her. Leela smiled.

"Let me call Sammy and make sure it's okay I take the whole week off." Clay was so happy he kissed her on the cheek and smiled.

"Thank you, Leela. Thank you." Alex was happy, too. He was worried about his sister. She was actually closer to him in D.C. than she was here.

Leela called Sammy who told her it was fine. She had heard about Leela's condition from Ashley and was surprised she hadn't noticed the symptoms sooner. Then Leela called Ashley to let her know she'd be gone and Ashley seemed happy for her. She told her to have lots of fun and that when she got back they'd get together. Two hours later Leela had packed and Clay had put her bags in the car and the three of them got ready to go. Alex hugged Leela for a long time, he was really sorry he'd lost touch with her.

"Why don't you guys come through Virginia on your way back and stop and see us?" Clay thought that was a good idea and agreed, and then they were off. Leela and Clay were headed toward his house and Alex was headed toward home.

Chapter 13

As they drove it occurred to Leela she had never been to his house before. She didn't even know where he lived, so she asked him about it.

"It's a house I bought from my great-grandmother right before she passed away," he told her. "She wanted it to stay in the family and everyone else had their own place. At that time I lived out of an apartment I was only too happy to give up." Leela smiled in her head as she pictured a little white house with a picket fence around the front yard, but when they pulled up to his house she was not ready for what she saw.

"Here we are. Home sweet home!" he said as he pulled into a long driveway off Devonshire Court. The driveway was about two blocks long and at the end of it stood a big brick house Leela had only read about in books.

"Oh my god, Clay, this is your house?" She was in awe. He could see that he hadn't remembered to prepare her for it. It was very elaborate but it hadn't cost him much since his great grandmother sold it to him for less than half of the market value.

"This is my home. And yours, too, someday, I hope." It was so beautiful that Leela didn't know what to say at first. There were flowers in the front of the house and neatly groomed bushes lining the drive. Big willow trees were in the front yard that were the size of a football field, and from the outside Leela thought there must have been twenty rooms in the house.

"Come on in. I'll give you the grand tour!" he said,

smiling at her. He unlocked the front door and she stepped into a large front room with beautiful antique furniture and very expensive paintings on the walls.

"This is so beautiful, Clay." Clay guided her into the next room, which was an elaborate dining room with a banquet table. "You must do a lot of entertaining?" she asked, but he shook his head.

"No, but my great grandmother and grandfather did all the time. Grandfather Warner was the president of the Palmside Federal Savings Bank."

The kitchen was off the dining room and it was huge. Leela had never seen a bigger kitchen, and it had any appliance you could have ever wanted. There was also a library and a den on the first floor, as well as two bedrooms. One of the rooms was used as a workout room, and had weightlifting equipment while the other had a twin bed and dresser. Leela could tell it was not often used. There was a bathroom downstairs, as well. On the top level there were four bedrooms. One was the master bedroom with an adjoining bathroom. Leela could tell that was Clay's room because she could see his clothes laid out neatly on his bed ready to be packed for D.C. The other bedrooms looked just like the guest room downstairs. Scarcely used. One room had a computer in it with books on the same subject. *He must work there*, she thought to herself. It was all so much that Leela hadn't realized that Clay was staring at her.

"Like it?" he asked her.

"It's beautiful, Clay. I didn't realize you were..." She wasn't sure what to say next. She thought the word rich was appropriate but she stopped herself because it didn't seem right to say.

"I'm not, Leela, it should be illegal. I paid such a small price for this. But it's still in the family. My great grandmother told me when she sold it to me that she knew I'd meet the perfect woman to fill the house again." Leela had tears in her eyes because she knew that he meant filling it with children, which she was sure she couldn't do. Clay could see she was upset and he realized what he had just said.

"Leela, all I want is you. Kids would be great but you are my dream, and I need you." She kissed him then and all he wanted to do was throw her on the bed and make love to her like they had the week before, but he knew she was still bruised and sore from her fall. Instead, he touched a hand to her bruised face and kissed her forehead.

After the grand tour, he packed his bags quickly and they locked up the house and started the drive to D.C.

"Leela, do you think you would move in with me when we get back?" Leela looked at him. Nothing should have surprised her since he had already asked her to marry him earlier in the day.

"What?" She couldn't imagine living in that huge house.

"Come on, Leela, you'll love it. I have plenty of room and you can decorate it any way you want. And there's a playhouse in the backyard I didn't show you. Ashley and Ryan can come over and play. And we can put a swing set back there for him. And," Leela had to stop him.

"Clay, let's take it slow, okay? Let's see how this week goes. Plus, I live close to the diner and your house is a long walk." Clay laughed. "Leela, I have another car parked in the garage you can use, or I can drive you. That is not going to work as an excuse for me." She smiled at him, hoping if she didn't continue the conversation he wouldn't either. He took the hint and didn't bring it up again the rest of the drive there.

"Where are we staying?" Leela asked as they entered D.C.

"The Clarion," Clay said. It was one of the more elegant hotels in D.C, and Leela had heard of it. He was spoiling her. When they pulled up to the hotel it was more beautiful than she could have imagined. He had reserved the honeymoon suite and the clerk at the desk assumed they had just gotten married. *They look like a handsome couple*, the clerk thought to himself. Even if Leela did have some bruises on her face, she was the most beautiful woman he had ever seen.

Their room was equally extravagant. There was a living room, a small kitchen with appliances, a big bathroom with a large hot tub, and a lovely bedroom with the most beautiful paintings on the wall Leela had ever seen. There was a big screen television in both the bedroom and living room equipped with DVD players, VCR's and surround sound. There were stereos in both rooms, as well. Leela was in heaven. "Are you hungry?" Clay asked Leela as they unpacked their bags.

"No, just tired," she replied. It was a long drive and she was still stiff from her fall.

"Let's watch a movie tonight. Your choice," Clay said, smiling at her.

She smiled back.

"That's a great idea." She wasn't ready to go out yet. She was hoping the bruises on her face faded soon.

After they unpacked, Leela called Alex to let him know that they had arrived on time, and she gave him her room number in case he wanted to get a hold of her. Then Leela and Clay settled down on the couch and watched a movie, holding each other. They both were so exhausted from the week before that they were asleep in no time.

Chapter 14

When Leela woke up on Monday morning Clay had already left for work, but not before leaving some and fresh bagels on the table in the kitchen. He had also left her a note saying he'd be back for lunch around noon. She smiled when she read it. It was nine-thirty and she had two and a half hours. She sat down at the table and ate two bagels, then went into the living room and turned on the radio to find a radio station she liked. It was playing oldies and it reminded her of when she and Alex were kids with their parents. She had thought about calling him then but knew he'd be at work, so instead she called the diner.

"Hi, Sammy, it's Leela. Is Ashley busy?" Sammy was glad to hear her voice. She had been worried after what she had heard over the weekend.

"Sure, Leela, and take it easy, okay? I want you back soon." Leela smiled.

"You, too, Sammy, take it easy and take care of that baby!" A minute later Ashley was on the phone.

"Leela, you okay?" Leela smiled.

"Yes, Ashley, this is the most beautiful hotel I've ever been in. And I feel good, too." Ashley was smiling. She was so happy for her. "That's great, girl. I got four tables going so can I call you later? What's your number?" Leela gave Ashley her number and they hung up. Leela just wanted to share this with someone and Ashley was her only friend.

It was ten-thirty before Leela walked into the bathroom with the huge tub. She filled it up with bubbles and climbed slowly in. She had taken a magazine with her and was going to relax while she had the chance. When Clay left after lunch she planned to explore a little. It was an hour before she climbed out and got dressed, and she felt great.

Clay called at eleven-thirty and asked Leela to meet him downstairs at the deli in the lobby. Leela got dressed in her jeans and a nice sweater and walked to the lobby. She saw the deli back in the corner, and when she arrived she was surprised to see Clay already there. He had even ordered for her and their food was just being brought to the table.

When he saw her he stood up and kissed her on her cheek. "Well, hello, my love. And how are you feeling this morning?" She looked at him with loving eyes.

"Wonderful, dear. I soaked in the pool in our bathroom for an hour and it felt good."

Clay laughed. "I'm jealous."

They sat down to begin to eat. He only had an hour but was dying to see her. They had a lovely lunch and he promised to be home by six, and she told him she was going to go out exploring. He looked a bit nervous given her condition, but she reassured him. He gave her his cell phone to carry just in case, knowing he could always be reached on the phone at the office. Forty-five minutes later he kissed her goodbye, and as he walked out the front hotel doors she walked back to her room thinking of just how lucky she was to have him.

Leela grabbed her purse and put the cell phone Clay had given her in it. He had also given her his credit card and told her to go buy something to wear to dinner tonight. Leela objected to the card, but he insisted so she finally gave in. There was no use fighting with him over it. As much as she didn't want to use it she knew it was a battle she wouldn't win. She knew he had plenty of money to spend on her and even though she was determined not to let him, he would, and she knew it. In the end he had told her that if she didn't go pick out a dress he would order one for her - and he was sure she'd like to pick one out herself.

As she walked through the lobby, one of the desk clerks greeted her as Ms. Warner. She was about to correct him but stopped, it kind of had a good sound to her. She was flattered and smiled back at him while waving. This was all new to her; no one had ever noticed her like that before.

She decided to stay close to the hotel today just to test her waters, and she had all week to go exploring farther. Clay had promised to take Wednesday off to take her sightseeing. There were several shops very close to the hotel and quite a few people shopping. She began to feel a bit out of place in her faded jeans as she watched well-dressed and business casual attired women browsing about with shopping bags in tow.

She passed up several stores because they just looked too fancy for her taste before stopping in front of a shop named *The Perfect Fit*. There were several plain yet elegant dresses in the front window that Leela adored, and when she walked in she fell in love with the entire store. She tried on several dresses before she found the one she wanted. It was a navy blue satin gown with three quarter length sleeves, and it fit her like a glove. She absolutely loved it, and knew Clay would too.

She almost cringed when she looked at the price tag, though. It was $75 and she hadn't paid that much for half her wardrobe. As she looked at the other dresses she realized they were all priced nearly twice as much and decided that it was worth it. If it were too much for Clay she'd pay him back. She had a credit card of her own and almost put it on hers, but knew Clay would get upset. She purchased the dress and again was called Ms. Warner since she was using his card.

She asked the sales woman where she could find a pair of shoes to match, who recommended another shop down the street. Leela started to walk out of the store when the woman asked her if she'd like the dress delivered to the hotel so she didn't have to carry it, and Leela agreed, thanking her. She was grateful.

Two blocks down Leela found the shop the woman from The Perfect Fit suggested, and was overwhelmed when she walked in and saw hundreds of pairs of shoes of all styles and colors. It took two sales ladies and forty-five minutes to help her find the right style and fit, and when she did she was relieved. Shopping for one outfit had been harder than she expected. But she finally paid the $50 for the pair of shoes that would perfectly compliment her dress, and she once again - reluctantly - put it on Clay's credit card. As before, the sales associate promised her she'd have the shoes delivered to the hotel within the hour.

It was quarter after three when Leela finished her outfit shopping and she knew that Clay wouldn't be home till six, and they wouldn't go to dinner until around seven if not later. She was excited now that she could just roam the streets and window shop at her leisure. The city was so beautiful and she was mesmerized by it. She walked through several antique shops on the strip and stopped at a small deli and rested while drinking a soda and eating a muffin.

At four she started back toward the hotel and noticed an antique shop she must have missed. As she walked through it she saw beautiful furniture and old china dolls before spying a section of old antique jewelry in the back. She fell instantly in love with a beautiful necklace with matching earrings and bracelet. The whole set was only twenty-five dollars and Leela knew it would look great with her new dress. It was silver and the necklace had a sterling silver heart on it.

This time she paid with her credit card and took it with her in her purse instead of having it delivered. She also saw a beautiful antique money clip she thought reminded her of Clay, so she bought it as well.

By five o'clock she was walking back through the hotel

lobby and the bellman advised her that her packages had been delivered to her room. She was surprised at first that they had gone into their room but then laughed, realizing they do it all the time and had a key. She thanked him and gave him a ten-dollar bill like she had seen Clay do the day before. He smiled at her in return.

When she got back into the room her dress and shoes were in the closet as promised by the bellman. As she stopped and admired the beautiful outfit for a moment, then took the jewelry out of her purse and laid it on the table next to the bed. She left the money clip in her purse, wrapped up so she could give it to Clay at dinner. She took a quick bath to relax and by quarter till six she was dressed in jeans again and sitting down watching television, waiting on Clay to return from work.

Just as promised, at six o'clock Clay walked through the door and gave her the biggest hug he could. He was worried about her out alone and he was relieved she was okay. She had missed him, and was starting to think she could get used to him coming home to her every night. That decision would have to wait, though, as she still had a lot to sort through.

After relaxing for an hour Clay asked Leela if she was ready for dinner. She hadn't eaten anything since lunch except a muffin, so she was famished. He asked her if she had gotten a dress and she nodded, hoping he wouldn't be upset at how much she had spent.

"Good, I'm going to go take a quick shower and you can get dressed while you wait. I can't wait to see you," he said, kissing her on the cheek before disappearing into the bathroom.

Twenty minutes later Clay walked out of the bathroom completely dressed in suit and tie, and he was stunned when he saw Leela. "Wow!" he said. He didn't know what else to say. The dress made her look so good, it was a perfect fit and she looked beautiful.

She blushed.

"Well," she said, "like it?"

He laughed. She knew he did. She had on her jewelry she'd bought that day and it went beautifully with the outfit. "Leela, you look great! I guess you had success finding the dress."

Leela looked guilty for a moment. "What's wrong?" he asked, afraid she wasn't feeling well again.

"It's just that I feel so guilty using your credit card for this. The dress was $75 and the shoes were $50. I paid for the jewelry myself, though."

He looked stunned and Leela suddenly thought he was mad at her for spending so much. "The dress was only seventy-five?" he asked. She thought he was being sarcastic and was about to tell him she'd give him the money back, when he began to laugh. "Leela, where'd you find it? Most stores around here don't sell dresses like that for less than two hundred dollars. You got a real deal!"

She laughed at herself for underestimating him. "I passed those shops up," she said. "I found this perfect shop called The Perfect Fit." He smiled at her. He loved her for all she was - honest and pure.

"And by the way, Leela, I'm giving you the money back for that jewelry. I'm taking away your credit card and you can only use mine. This trip was my idea and I pay for everything. You can buy anything you want, Leela, whatever your heart desires. No matter how much money, it's not an issue. But you must use my card." She was about to disagree when he took her purse, pulled out her card and put in it his wallet.

"Whatever you say, sir," was her response to him as he embraced her, giving her a long and hard kiss.

They took a cab to a little restaurant Clay had picked out called The Lighthouse. It was a beautiful place, and the food was delicious. Leela looked so gorgeous that as they walked in, several people stopped to look at her. They made a handsome couple and the wait staff assumed they were married, so she was called Ms. Warner all night.

Neither of them corrected anyone, as Clay was hoping she would marry him, and although Leela was getting used to the idea she just didn't think it was fair to Clay - and wasn't ready to agree yet.

After they ate and had ordered dessert, Leela pulled her purse onto her lap.

"Clay, I know you don't want this but I bought you a present today." Clay looked surprised, he hadn't expected that at all.

"Leela, you didn't have to," was all he said. He was secretly anxious to see what it was and as she handed him the little wrapped box he smiled at her. No matter what it was he knew he'd love it, and when he opened it his eyes lit up.

"Leela, this is great. I love it." She could tell he really did. He leaned over and kissed her cheek.

"Leela, I have a confession for you," Clay said, looking guilty.

"What?" Leela said. She was completely confused.

"I have a present for you, too," he said as he handed her a little velvet box. Leela looked up, shocked. She was pretty sure she knew what it was, and was too nervous to open it because she didn't know what she'd say.

"Open it!" he said excitedly. She finally forced her fingers to open the box, and in it was a beautiful - and large - diamond ring.

"Leela, will you please marry me! I love you with all my heart and I want to spend the rest of our lives together. No matter what the future brings, I want to spend it with you." As Leela sat there, staring at the ring she was holding, she felt her head nodding yes. She looked up at Clay with tears in her eyes because she just couldn't say no to him.

"Clay, I will, I just hope you understand what you're getting into." Then Clay let out a shout of glee and put his arms around her, kissing her with passion.

Leela was admiring the ring as Clay took it out of the

box and slipped it on her finger. It was a perfect fit. It was an antique white gold band with a four-karat diamond, surrounded by several smaller diamond clusters. It was a near perfect match for they jewelry she had purchased earlier in the day.

"I love you so much, Leela!" Clay said, as he looked her in the eyes.

"I love you, too, Clay." Leela wasn't sure what else to say. She was completely overwhelmed by this, and was still in shock as the waiter poured them champagne.

They stayed at the restaurant for another hour, talking and drinking champagne. Leela was feeling a little tipsy as Clay took care of the check, and when he was done he pulled her chair out for her. The hotel was only a few blocks away so they decided to walk and enjoy the beautiful night.

Twenty minutes later when they walked into their hotel room, Clay gently undressed her and they made love to celebrate the decision to spend the rest of their lives together.

Chapter 15

The next morning Leela woke up as Clay was getting dressed. It was seven-thirty and he wouldn't leave for work until eight.

"Good morning, sweetheart!" he said as he leaned over the bed and kissed her forehead.

"Morning," she said, recalling the night before and looked at her ring finger.

"Oh my, it's real. I thought I was dreaming. We really are engaged." She smiled up at him and he laughed at her.

"Yes, my dear, we are. I'm taking you out to dinner again tonight, so go find yourself another bargain dress today. As a matter of a fact, buy two or three. You'll need them." Leela laughed at him being so serious. So she didn't comment back except to nod her head.

"Will you meet me for lunch?" she asked. She hoped he would. She loved seeing him now and didn't want him to leave her.

"Sure, hotel lobby?" he asked.

"Actually, I stopped at this great deli yesterday we should try. It had an interesting menu. It was on Tenth and Main."

Clay smiled. "Anything for you, my love. I'll be there at noon." Then he kissed her gently and left for work.

Leela called Ashley at home as soon as Clay left. She knew she'd still be home and was dying to tell her about the ring.

"Ashley, he asked me to marry him!" Leela cried as Ashley answered the phone.

"Leela, oh my god, that's great, you said yes, right?" Ashley seriously wondered since she knew of Leela's condition.

"Yes, I said yes. He gave me this huge ring that weighs a ton and took me to this fancy restaurant. I couldn't say no." Ashley couldn't contain her smile, she was so happy for Leela. Leela let Ashley go, and promised to call her again soon, then called Alex at his office. His assistant said he was in a meeting, so Leela left him a message with Clay's cell phone number. She asked her to tell him it wasn't an emergency and not to worry, just call when he got a chance. She was eager to tell him about the engagement. Sadly Leela realized she had no one else to call and tell, but at least she had Alex back.

Leela took a long bubble bath to sooth away sore muscles brought on by all the previous day's walking, and a glance in the mirror beforehand showed her bruises to be fading. No matter how sore she was, nothing was going to keep her from going out again today. She had more shopping to do - and this time she was actually excited about it.

She planned on going back to the same dress shop as the day before, and also wanted to venture out a little farther to see what else she could find. Clay had assured her that she could not max out his credit card no matter how much she spent, and told her to get whatever she wanted. He encouraged her to do so with so much energy that she had finally given in. She had never been spoiled like this before and she had to admit, she was enjoying it.

By ten o'clock Leela was walking out of the hotel lobby and into the hustle of the busy shopping strip. She reached all the expensive stores she had passed up the day before and decided to go in just for fun. As she looked around, she realized that Clay had been right. She could have bought four of the dresses from yesterday and it still would be less expensive than one of these. She honestly didn't like the style of the more expensive dresses, she thought they looked like something someone stuck up would wear. Leela had almost made it to her favorite dress shop when Clay's cell phone rang.

"Hello?" she answered, hoping it was Clay.

"Leela? Is everything all right? I just got your message." Leela smiled. It was Alex.

"Yes, I'm fine. Just out wandering around Washington D.C. How are you?" she asked. She couldn't wait to tell him about her news.

"I'm good. Laura has been sick lately. I think the flu. But we're good other than that. Enjoying yourself?" He already knew Clay was going to propose, he just didn't know when. Clay had called him to ask his permission since she had no living parents, and Alex had easily given his blessing.

"Yes, actually," she said happily. "Alex, Clay asked me to marry him last night." Alex was quiet; he wasn't sure how she had answered.

"What'd you say?" he asked after he realized she wasn't volunteering anything more.

"I said yes," she said softly.

"Thank God!" Alex cried. He was so happy for her. "Leela, that is great. Actually, I knew he was proposing this week, he called me to ask for my blessing. I think it is a great idea and he loves you so much. You both deserve to be happy." Leela was smiling but still had a feeling of guilt.

"But Alex, what about the condition? I feel like I am cheating him on life." Alex quickly sobered up, he was not going to let her feel that way.

"Leela, you deserve a happy life. He can give it to you. No matter what happens this is what he wants. I know because I had a very long talk with him about it yesterday." Leela was surprised to hear that they had talked, especially about that, but she knew it needed to be done. She couldn't convince Clay of the hardships a life with her might entail, and was glad Alex had talked with Clay about it.

They talked for about ten minutes more and then Alex had to get back to work. She told him to give Laura her love and tell her she hoped she felt better.

Leela walked into her dress shop and was pleasantly surprised to find the woman that had helped her the day before remembered her. "Ms. Warner, was everything okay with your dress?" she asked, concerned.

Leela smiled at her.

"Yes, it was great. I'm actually here for more. I would like something in black, maybe red, and maybe something off-white, too." The sales lady smiled, Leela's small town friendliness was such a change from her more metropolitan patrons.

Within an hour Leela had picked out three more beautiful dresses and paid for them with Clay's card. This time the bill came to $260 but she knew it was a good deal - considering the dresses she had seen at the other shops. She had them sent to the hotel just like the day before.

She hit the shoe store next and bought a pair of black shoes to match both the red and black dress, and then she picked out a pair of off-white shoes to match the off-white dress. She had those sent to the hotel, too. When she looked at her watch, she realized it was time to start toward the deli to meet Clay. It was only five minutes away. Clay arrived at the deli at about the same time Leela. He smiled the minute he saw her.

"Well, hey there, beautiful. Looking for me?" he said in his country drawl.

"Well, as a matter of a fact I am," she said back as he kissed her.

"I've missed you, Leela," he said as they walked to the counter to order their food.

"Do any shopping yet?" he asked. Leela laughed.

"Actually, I've maxed out your card now." Clay laughed knowing that wasn't likely.

"Great, I'm glad, what'd you get?" She was enthralled by the fact that he seemed interested in everything she did.

"I bought three more dresses and two pairs of shoes. Dresses were $260 together and the shoes were $75. Is that okay?" Clay grabbed his chest jokingly.

"My god, woman! You're going to bankrupt me!" She laughed, knowing he was kidding. "Actually, darling, I hope you shop all day. Buy yourself a new wardrobe, jeans, sweats, books, anything your heart desires. That card was designed especially for you." She blushed, still not used to his generosity.

"You are too kind, sir," she said with an impish smile.

They had a nice lunch that seemed over all too soon. Clay regretted having to leave her to return to work, but promised to be off by six as they had an eight o'clock dinner reservation.

Before he left, Clay told Leela about a shopping center downtown that might interest her, and suggested she take a cab there. He gave her plenty of cash for whatever she couldn't pay for with the card. Leela had five hours to do whatever she wanted and shopping sounded good to her. She wasn't thrilled about spending all his money, but she loved to browse anyway.

Clay was right - the shops downtown were much more interesting to Leela. She walked through several bookstores and picked up a few books she had wanted to read. Then she went into the mall there and found a pair of jeans as well as a sweater she really liked. She also bought a few new bras to go with her new dresses.

This time she hadn't sent anything back to the hotel, figuring she'd stop buying when her hands got full. The more she looked the more things she found, but in the end she buy anything else. She wasn't feeling so hot either, so she got a cab and headed back to the hotel.

By the time she reached the hotel Leela was looking pale. The doorman saw that she looked ill and carried her bags up to her room for her. She was grateful and tipped him again like before. She hadn't even bothered to put her new clothes away; she just went to the couch to lie down.

Although she hadn't meant to fall asleep, she was startled awake by the phone ringing. She looked at the clock and it was five-thirty.

"Hello?" Leela answered, still half asleep.

"Leela? It's Laura. How are you? Are you okay?" Leela instantly wondered if Alex was okay. Laura had never called her before.

"Yeah, I'm fine. Just shopped all day and was tired. How are you? Alex said this morning you were sick." Leela didn't want to just come out and say, "What do you want." She actually enjoyed talking to Laura, but was still afraid something was wrong.

"Actually, I'm okay now. It must have been the flu. Alex called me and told me you and Clay got engaged. That's great! I just wanted to congratulate you." Leela smiled with relief, nothing was wrong.

"Thanks, Laura. I'm still so nervous, I hope this is the right thing to do. I do love him, though." Laura knew exactly what she was talking about and felt the same way Alex did. They had a right to a happy life together no matter how long it may be.

"It is, Leela. You both deserve it. I'm thinking of coming to D.C. on Thursday to do shopping for my bridesmaids' dresses. I was hoping you'd join me since you are one of the two I'll have."

Leela was thrilled. "Laura, that's great. I'd love to. It will give me someone to talk to while Clay is at work."

Laura told her what time she'd be in and they hung up. Laura and Leela hadn't spent time together alone, and both were excited to finally get to know each other better.

Between the nap and the phone call Leela only had twenty minutes before Clay would get home, so she rushed to take a shower. When he walked in the door this at quarter after six, she was ready but the dress. She was feeling much better than she had been before her nap, so decided not to bother Clay with her small episode.

He was happy to hear she had gone shopping for

herself again, but disappointed she hadn't bought more. She showed him what she bought as he lay on the bed - looking at more than just her new clothes.

"Leela, I love you," was all he could say before he pulled her onto the bed with him for a lovemaking session. By the time they got up again it was time to get dressed for dinner.

Dinner that night was very elegant, and Leela struck quite a figure in her new black dress. Clay could hardly keep his eyes off her all night, no matter how great she looked he seemed to see something hanging over her. She looked like she didn't feel as good as she had the day before, and he wondered if perhaps she had overdone it with the full day out shopping.

That night they talked about Alex and Laura. Clay was thrilled that Laura was going to spend the day with Leela on Thursday. He had a growing concern that Leela might overtax herself, and having Laura in town eased his mind. They spent a wonderful evening talking about inconsequential things, and they both regretted it when it was time to go back to the hotel.

They made the trip back without incident, but when they got to the room Leela felt the now familiar dark cloud come over her. By the time they got to bed, Leela felt the darkness take over as her illness pushed her to unconsciousness. Clay never realized the difference as he drifted off to sleep holding the woman he loved.

Chapter 16

Since Clay didn't have in the morning, both of them slept in until nine o'clock. Clay called and had room service bring up a big breakfast, which ended up being too much for Leela to eat. Their plan for the day was to take it easy in the hotel room until lunch, then go see some museums, and Leela wanted to see the White House.

Clay had found an old movie on TV that they watched and then played cards until lunch. Leela felt so comfortable with him that she knew there could be no lies between them, she would have to tell him the truth in order for their relationship to work.

"Clay," Leela said, "Yesterday, after shopping, I had to come home and take a nap because I got dizzy and felt faint. Last night I think I passed out instead of falling asleep." Leela had tears in her eyes as she told him, and Clay pulled her close.

"Leela, I know we're going to have times like that. I completely understand. This is the life I want and if it means catching you when you fall, by God I'll be there." He held her for a long time while she gazed at the ring on her finger.

They decided to go find a diner for lunch and then go to the museum. Clay thought maybe they should have just stayed at the hotel, but Leela assured him that she was fine, and really felt like she was. She felt so light and happy seeing the nation's capital with him.

They found a diner that much like the one Leela herself worked in, although the food there was much better she thought. Then they went to the museum and then an art gallery across the street. Later in the day Clay drove her to the White House, and she thought it was beautiful. They sat in front and talked for a long time, and the same thoughts kept flowing through her mind. She was really going to marry this guy, and she had never been happier in all her life.

It was six o'clock before they got back to the hotel, and Leela told Clay she didn't want to do a fancy dinner again, so they just ordered room service and watched a romance on the television.

They had a better night in than they could have had going out. She felt so comfortable listening as he told her stories about his childhood and Laura and his sister. He told Leela that when they got back to Palmside she'd have to meet his family. Only his mom and sister were alive. His sister would be the other bridesmaid in Laura's wedding. Leela talked about her family when she was little and how they had been so happy. She missed her parents deeply and Clay could tell.

"Do you want Alex to walk you down the aisle?" Clay asked out of the blue. Leela hadn't really thought about it.

"I guess there is no one else, is there?" she said sadly. Clay wanted to cheer her up, he hadn't meant to make her sad.

"Have you given any thought to when you want to get married?" Leela thought about for a moment.

"I'd like to get Alex and Laura off and married first. Do you mind waiting a little while?" Clay smiled. She was always thinking of everyone else.

"That's fine," he said, then laughing he said, "How about the next day?" She laughed and told him she'd really think about it.

"Do you want a big wedding or a small wedding?" That one was easy for Leela to answer.

"Well, given that I can count all my friends on one hand it will be up to you how many people you want to invite. I'd be happy with a small wedding. But if you want a big one that is okay with me, too." *There she goes again*, he thought to himself, *catering to everyone else*.

"We'll decide that later," he said in answer. The rest of the night went without incident for Leela, which she was grateful for. Clay was just sorry he had to go back to work the next day. He only had two more days to work in D.C. then they could go home and start their life together. His replacement was already there, which was how he got the day off. He was still training him, but would be done by the end of week.

Clay wanted to ask if she was moving in with him when they got home, but he didn't want to ruin the good mood if she said not yet. He'd approach that subject with her tomorrow. He desperately wanted her to. While holding her in bed that night after they made love, it was all he could think about, spending his life with her.

Leela was waiting for Laura in the lobby when she arrived the next morning around ten. Leela had felt good, and was looking forward to going shopping with her soon to be sister-in-law.

"Hi, Leela. You look good today." Leela couldn't help but hug Laura, she already felt like family. The truth was Leela didn't have much family left, so she was delighted to have Laura. Leela took Laura up to the suite to put down some bags she had brought, and then they sat and talked about Laura's plans for the wedding - and what she needed to accomplish in D.C.

"So, when are you planning on getting married?" Laura asked her. Leela thought for a minute, she knew that Laura's wedding was in a few months and she didn't want to do anything until after that.

"I'm not sure, maybe in the fall? Definitely not 'till you and Alex are settled in."

Laura gave Leela a serious look. "Leela, my wedding is in two and a half months. I know that Clay is anxious about this whole thing. You don't need to put anything off because of my wedding!"

Leela laughed nervously. "No, I'm just nervous myself. I still can't believe this is happening." Laura smiled at her. She really had loved Leela from the moment she met her, and was thrilled that her childhood friend Clay was so happy with her. She couldn't believe Alex had gone so long without talking to her.

They left the hotel and took a cab to the shopping strip Leela had gone to on Tuesday. There was a bridal shop there that Laura wanted to see. She wanted to pick out flowers, Unity candles, and bridesmaid dresses. Laura had decided she wanted her colors red and silver and was hoping to find some flowers to compliment it, possibly even red roses.

By the time they left the bridal shop they had purchased some candles and decorations Laura had fell in love with the moment she saw them, then it was off to a dress shop. First, though, they wanted to get some lunch.

Leela took her to the diner her and Clay had eaten at the day before because she had been impressed by it, and the two had a nice talk over lunch.

"I know this great little dress shop that I have bought a few dresses at this week that I'm sure have something nice. We could look there. Clay says their prices are much better than the trendy shops." Laura was thankful, the wedding was starting to get expensive and she had wanted to buy the bridesmaid dresses since there were only two of them. As the women walked into the dress shop, the sales lady instantly smiled when she noticed Leela.

"Back again? You must be some senator's wife to need all these new dresses this week." Laura laughed because she couldn't believe Leela had been there that much.

"Actually," Leela replied with a smile, "my future sister-in-law needs two matching dresses for her bridesmaids. I am one of them. Her colors are red and silver." The sales lady smiled at the girls and told them she'd be right back.

An hour later, Laura had found the perfect dress. They

were actually red and silver and looked great on Leela. Laura knew it would look good on Clay's sister Patricia, too, as they were close to the same size. Leela asked the sales woman to have them sent to her room like the other times she had been there.

"Wow, Leela, I've really gotten a lot done today and I'm so glad I came. I don't have to be back home for several hours and we only have to go to the flower shop now, so do you want to go see some more sights?"

"Actually, I don't know what else there is. Let's go the flower shop and see what we find on the way." The two ladies walked happily down Tenth Street, window-shopping at almost every store.

"Laura, I'm so happy you came into my brother's life. I'm not sure if he would have ever called me if you hadn't." Laura looked at Leela with sadness. She could only imagine how lonely it had been for her.

"He would have, trust me. He missed you dearly." Leela just smiled at her, not knowing what else to say.

After Laura spent an hour or so picking out flowers, the ladies headed back to the hotel and sat in the bar and had a drink. "I'm coming to Palmside next weekend to set up the reception hall. I thought maybe you could have lunch with Patricia and me. You know, give you a chance to get to know her. By the way, when does Clay plan on introducing you to his family?" Leela laughed at her.

"I'm not sure they even know we're engaged yet."

Laura laughed at her. "They know."

An hour later the ladies were saying goodbye. Leela asked Laura to say hello to Alex for her, and reassure him she was fine. Laura promised to, and Leela smiled as she watched Laura leave. She really enjoyed the day.

Clay came home at six o'clock and they had plans for dinner later, so she decided to wear the new red dress. She thought it looked very sexy, and Clay was taking her dancing after dinner - if she felt up to it.

When Clay came out of the bathroom dressed in a

handsome suit, he was stunned at how great Leela looked.

"Oh my God, maybe we ought to just stay in," he said with a mischievous grin on his face.

"No way, Mr. Warner. You're taking me dancing." She was actually very excited about the prospect of getting on the dance floor with him.

Dinner was better than Leela had hoped and she felt so lively that she practically begged Clay to take her dancing. He gladly gave in and they went to a place called Maxine's and danced all night long. Leela had never been anywhere like it. The place was a beautiful club, and the dance floor was always packed. Here and there about the crowd Leela recognized a few congressman and other political figures.

By midnight Clay knew it was time to go, as he had to be at work the next morning. Tomorrow was Friday and he had to finish up all his loose ends so they could go home. Reluctantly Leela agreed. As they had their last dance at Maxine's, she saw a flash and was surprised to find a reporter had just taken their picture. Clay told her not to worry, once they realized they weren't famous the photographer would just trash it. Leela just smiled and they headed for the hotel in a cab.

Chapter 17

Leela had nothing to do on Friday when she woke up. It was Clay's last day working in Washington and although he had hoped to finish early, hadn't made her any promises. She was tired of shopping and decided to spend the day relaxing. She was exhausted from the night before, she had never been dancing like that and had loved every minute of it. When she picked up the morning paper and flipped through it, she noticed her picture in the entertainment section.

It was a great picture of her dancing with Clay, looking like two lovers who saw nothing around them except each other. Leela laughed as she read the article. Apparently they had done a piece on Maxine's due to its recent popularity and the two had been the perfect perception of what they wanted to display. Leela was flattered and couldn't wait to show Clay. She was going to get a few more copies to keep.

After reading the paper, Leela took a long hot bubble bath and relaxed. She had picked up a novel a few days before and decided to start reading it. After a while she noticed her skin was starting to prune up so she got out of the bathtub, put on her robe and went to the bedroom and lay on the bed to continue reading. It was about noon and Leela wasn't hungry for lunch yet so she just started to read. It only took ten minutes for Leela to fall asleep still holding her book in her hands.

It was two-thirty when Leela finally woke back up, she had been exhausted and needed the nap. Leela went to the small kitchen and took some fresh fruit out of the refrigerator for a snack, and the phone rang shortly after she finished eating, She was thrilled to hear it was Alex on the other end.

"Hey, sis, I hear you and my wife-to-be had a wonderful time yesterday." Leela smiled at hearing his voice.

"Yes, we did, Alex. She's a great girl, you did good with her." Alex laughed.

"You didn't do so bad yourself, Leela. By the way, I saw the D.C. paper today. Did you?" Leela blushed, she knew what he was referring to.

"Yes, I did. We went dancing last night."

"I can see that, sis. And you looked great and like you had a good time, too." Leela smiled.

"I did." They talked briefly about Maxine's and then Alex asked if they were coming to his house, still, on their way home. Leela told him they would, and they should be there around noon. The plan was to have lunch there and head back after a few hours. He gave her directions and they hung up.

Leela settled back down on the couch with her book again and read until Clay walked in the door at four-thirty.

"Hey there, darling," he said as he kissed her on the cheek.

"Hi, honey. Finished up?" She was hoping he was. She wanted to relax with him for a few hours and have dinner at a nice restaurant before they left.

"See the paper today?" she asked. He shook his head no, he had been busy trying to finish his work so he could get home early. He wanted to spend quality time with her, too.

She handed him the paper and as he saw the picture he laughed.

"I guess they don't trash the ones of normal everyday people anymore."

"I'd like to have another copy for a keepsake, Clay.

Let's get one when we go out tonight." Clay agreed and then called the hotel manager, asking if he could get them a couple copies. For the next few hours they talked and watched some TV, and Clay decided it was time to ask.

"Leela, will you move in with me when we get back?" Leela went quiet. She knew that it wasn't going to be long before he'd ask her that and she herself had been thinking about it. It was such a nice, beautiful house, but she was still reluctant.

"What about my apartment, Clay?" It was a valid question. She had a lease and wasn't sure if she could get out of it. However, she had lived there for a while and only had three more months on her lease.

"Maybe I can get him to forgive it?" Clay said thoughtfully.

"Clay, I only have three more months on it. Maybe we can just wait until then." Clay didn't want to wait. He wanted her there with him.

"Leela, I really want you to move in with me. I can't force you, but I would love it." She knew he wanted it badly so she agreed to talk to the landlord when they got home. Then she surprised him with her next comment.

"Let's get married in the fall." She had been thinking about it. "I'd love an October wedding. Outside with leaves on the ground all around us." Clay was so shocked to hear her actually planning their wedding, he was sure she'd never agree to that; all he could do was nod his head. She noticed he didn't comment and thought he didn't like the idea.

"But if that's not what you want..." Clay was quick to reassure her.

"No, Leela, that sounds great. I'd love that, too. And it's six months away so we have plenty of time to plan." What he didn't know is that when she was out shopping with Laura the day before she had already decided a lot of things.

"I'd like the colors to be fall colors. Oranges and reds -

like turning leaves.

I'd like my dress to be slim with no ruffles. I don't like ruffles. Sleeveless. I'll wear a sheer scarf around my shoulders." Clay couldn't believe his ears. When he looked at her he saw she had tears in her eyes. She had finally accepted the life they'd have and decided to give it her all. They relaxed for a little while longer, chatting about their wedding, and then decided it was time to get ready for dinner. This time she wore the off-white dress that Clay thought was very elegant, and just to show her he took her to the most elegant place in Washington.

They had a lovely dinner and when they got back to the hotel later that night he made love to her, knowing he had finally won her over. From that point on, he knew that whatever he did with his life would include her. He loved her more than he could have told her, so he just chose to show her.

As much as she tried to fight it, she felt herself falling into love more than she could explain, too. She'd never forget the week she spent in the capital with Clay. She would have the newspaper article to always remind her.

Saturday morning Leela packed up their bags and they ate breakfast one last time in the little kitchen in their hotel suite. By nine o'clock the car was loaded and they started their journey to Virginia to see Alex and Laura.

The drive didn't take them as long as planned and they pulled up into Alex's driveway at eleven. Alex must have seen them because he was coming out the front door as they got out of the car. He grabbed Leela and gave her a big hug and then shook Clay's hand. Laura met them at the door. Alex had a beautiful house, and as Laura gave them the tour Leela realized that they already had a room ready for a baby. Laura told her they were going to try to get pregnant right after the wedding. And it pained Leela to realize that she wouldn't get to do that. Laura immediately saw her reaction and changed the subject.

They had a nice lunch and Leela shared the ideas she

had for the wedding she wanted. Laura thought October was a perfect idea and loved her idea of the fall colors.

Reluctantly, three hours after they had arrived, Clay announced that they had better get going. He wanted Leela to spend the night at his house that night and still needed to ask her, and they would have to go by her apartment and get some things. Plus, he had noticed that even though he could tell Leela loved seeing her brother and enjoyed the visit, there was something bothering her. And once they were in the car and on the road Clay asked her.

"Leela, what is wrong? I know something is." Leela shook her head.

"No, honey, nothing is wrong. I just got a bit tired." Even though he thought there was more to it, he decided to let it go. A couple hours later he pulled up to the curb in front of her apartment.

"Leela, can we stay at my place tonight?" Leela looked at him and was about to say no when she decided she might as well see how she liked it.

"Sure, let's just get some things and put some of my dresses up. They are too nice for Palmside," she said, laughing.

They took all her bags up to her apartment and Clay sat on her couch resting while she packed a few things to take to his house.

"Take enough for the weekend," he told her, which was really just the next day, although he was hoping she would stay longer. In the end she only had one duffel bag with two pairs of jeans, two sweatshirts, two tee shirts, socks, panties, and a pair of pajamas.

"Do you need me to bring anything else?" she asked. Not sure if she had everything, she quickly grabbed her shampoo and toothbrush and they were on their way.

They stopped by the grocery store and picked up some groceries, and it was dark by the time they got back to his house. It looked even bigger this time when she walked up to the front door. He was carrying her bag and promised to get the groceries after the door was unlocked. When she walked in she wasn't sure where to go first.

"I'll put my clothes up in your room. Put the groceries away and I'll come down and fix some dinner."

She was upstairs for about fifteen minutes. She put her clothes in an empty drawer he had in his dresser and then sat on the bed looking around the room. It was so big and nice. That one room was probably half of her small apartment and she wondered if she would get used to it. As she walked by one of the spare bedrooms on the way downstairs, she couldn't help but think of the room Alex and Laura had ready for the baby they hoped to conceive soon. That would have been the perfect room - if only it were possible.

When she finally got back downstairs to the kitchen Clay had already started dinner. He was making one of his favorites, spaghetti. He was browning the beef while she started on the garlic bread. His kitchen was so roomy that she almost felt lost. There was a table in the corner that she sat at while watching the sauce bubble.

"I could get used to this," she said to Clay, trying to get her mind off the baby issue.

"Good, I hope you do," Clay said back happily. When dinner was ready they ate in the big dining room that had a table big enough for them and ten guests. She loved the house, and she loved him.

The next day Leela and Clay stayed around the house. They had a busy week and they were both tired. Leela was going back to work the next day and hoped that since she was mostly incident free for the last week that it was a good sign. She was going to the clinic the next morning to see the vampires again and hoped things hadn't progressed in the week. She actually felt good about it this time, and she finally had something worth living and fighting for.

Clay had taken her for a walk around his property and she thought it was a lovely place. She loved the small house in the backyard, but wasn't sure what purpose it would serve for them. Then he showed her the extra car he kept in the garage. It was a silver ford Taurus in immaculate condition. It had been sitting for nearly two years, only being driven occasionally.

"Wow, Clay, it's great." Clay had been sure she'd like it.

"Good, because it's yours, dear." Leela hadn't driven in years, but was sure she would pick it right back up. They went for a drive so Leela could get used to her new car.

"Now the diner isn't an excuse anymore," Clay told her, and she just smiled.

That night Leela called Ashley and talked to her for a long time. Ashley couldn't believe Leela's good fortune with Clay and was relieved to hear she hadn't had any more episodes. Leela promised to pick her up for work the next day and Ashley was glad.

That night Clay made dinner for Leela and they watched TV until they went to bed. They both had to work the next day and needed their sleep. As Clay lay in bed he couldn't believe Leela was there with him in his house - now their house. He couldn't have been happier.

Chapter 18

After Leela went to the clinic she drove to Ashley's apartment. They then drove Ryan to school and headed toward the diner.

"So, are you moving in with him?" Leela hadn't come out and told Ashley that she was thinking about it, but Ashley knew.

"Maybe," Leela answered.

"I think you should, Leela," Ashley pushed and Leela smiled at her.

"We're going to get married in October."

Ashley looked stunned. She hadn't expected Leela to agree to get married so soon. But she was thrilled. "That's great!" she said.

"Will you be my maid of honor?" Leela asked. She had already asked Laura to be her bridesmaid, too.

"I'd love to, Leela. I'm so happy for you!"

Monday the diner was busy as usual. Sammy was glad Leela was back and looking like she was feeling much better. She saw a light in her eyes that hadn't been there before, and she knew it was due to her new fiancé. She was happy for Leela, and it seemed so natural that it never occurred to anyone to think it strange that it hadn't been that long. They could see how much Leela was in love - and could see the same thing in Clay when he came to the diner to have lunch that day.

"Hello, beautiful! Have time for lunch with me?" Leela turned around; knowing who it was without looking.

"Give me ten minutes?" she asked. He nodded and sat down at the counter to wait. Just as promised, ten minutes later Leela sat down with him and they ordered lunch and talked. Clay told her how work was going, and she told him how good it felt to be back at the diner.

"Are you coming back to my place after work tonight?" he asked, hopeful.

"I need some more things from my house first. I'll stop by there on the way." Clay was thrilled, it looked like she was adjusting fast and he couldn't have been happier.

When their shift ended, Leela drove Ashley home and asked her if she would join them for dinner the following night, letting her know that Ryan was obviously invited, too. Ashley accepted the invitation, she was dying to see Clay's home that Leela had told her so much about.

Leela drove to her little apartment, which now that she looked at it was no bigger than the hotel room she'd stayed in. She came inside and realized that her answering machine was flashing.

"*You have two new messages...Message one...*Ms. Jacobs, this is Paulina at Dr. Risinger's office. Could you please give me a call? Thank you. I'll be in the office until six-thirty P.M."

Leela stopped dead in her tracks. She had been grabbing things around the house while she listened and now she stood still - what could they possibly want? She suddenly had a fear that it had gotten worse. She looked at the clock and it read five-twenty, so she picked up the phone and called Paulina.

"Yes, this is Leela Jacobs, I'm returning Paulina's call," she told the lady who answered the phone. After a few seconds of silence Paulina came on the phone.

"Leela, this is Paulina. I am so sorry to do this but we must have mixed up your results today with someone else's. They aren't consistent. Can you come back tomorrow morning?" Leela sighed a breath of relief, it hadn't gotten worse.

"Sure, I'll be there first thing tomorrow morning."

"Thanks, and I'm sorry about this. I'm not sure what happened." The two ladies hung up the phone.

The second message had been Clay telling her he picked up something for dinner so not to worry about it. This time when Leela packed her bag she packed enough for the week, which wasn't much since she wore a uniform to work. Then she grabbed a few things she loved, like the picture of her family and some odds and ends. She decided, since Clay wanted her to stay with him, he wouldn't mind if she made herself at home. She had decided to talk to her landlord the following day about the lease.

When she pulled up to Clay's house it had a great sense of home. He was waiting at the door for her and smiling. She started to grab her bags out of the car, motioning for her to put them down and telling her he would get them. He carried her bags upstairs and was pleased to see how much she had brought.

They made dinner together again that night and Leela told him about inviting Ashley and Ryan over the next night. Clay thought that was a great idea. After eating dinner and cleaning the kitchen, they cuddled up in the big living room in front of the big screen TV and watched a movie. By ten o'clock they were both tired and went to bed.

As promised, Leela went back to the clinic in the morning and once again let the vampires take her blood. It was a routine she was well used to by now. She stopped and picked up Ashley on her way to the diner and the two of them headed to work. Leela was excited about their dinner plans and Ashley was, too.

The day at the diner was busier than normal. Leela felt like she had just walked in the door when Clay came to meet her for lunch at eleven- thirty. She was delighted to see him. They sat down and had a nice lunch and talked about what they'd make for dinner that night. Leela wanted to make sure they had something Ryan liked. In the end they decided on barbecue chicken breasts and some side items and when Leela ran it by Ashley later that day she thought that sounded great.

After work Leela and Ashley drove to Ashley's apartment so she could change clothes and then they went to pick Ryan up from the day care. The three of them arrived at Clay's house at almost six o'clock and he already had the grill going. They went out back and showed Ryan the small playhouse, which he loved. Clay promised him they'd have a swing set next time he came to visit and Leela and Ashley laughed at him. Clay was so good with him and Leela felt guilty again for not being able to give him a baby.

While Clay and Ryan manned the grill, Leela gave Ashley the grand tour of the house. Ashley was just as stunned by it as Leela had been her first time.

"Man, looks like you struck gold," Ashley teased Leela. As far as Leela was concerned, she struck gold the minute she met Clay. He was so good to her.

Dinner was lively and the chicken was delicious. Leela had made corn on the cob and mashed potatoes and it was a dinner Ryan loved. By the time it was gone, Ryan had barbecue all over his face and Clay was teasing him. At nine o'clock Clay drove them home while Leela cleaned the kitchen.

"It was great having them over, wasn't it?" Leela said to Clay when he got back.

"Yes, it was. Ryan is such a great kid," he answered. Leela was quiet for a minute.

"I'm sorry I can't have kids, Clay," she said with tears in her eyes.

"Oh, baby, all I need is you. Don't worry about that. We have Ryan, and I'm sure that Alex and Laura will have kids soon." Leela smiled. That she knew would happen. Even though it didn't make her feel any better, she accepted it.

"We could always adopt," Clay said to Leela. It was an option she had never considered.

"It wouldn't be fair to adopt a baby, then die," she said bluntly. Clay was a little taken back by her comment.

"Leela, you could live a long life. You're selling yourself short again." It upset him when she talked like that. He decided it was time to go to her next doctor's appointment with her - to find out all the details on how she can live a better life.

"I'm just saying, Clay." Clay shook his head.

"I know what you're saying and I don't think you're being fair to yourself. Forget what I want and think about what you'd want if you weren't sick." Leela knew that it was pointless to think about what she'd want then. It wasn't going to happen.

"Clay, I just don't want to give myself, or you, false hope. Maybe we shouldn't get married if you want a baby so badly." Clay couldn't win no matter what he said.

"Leela, I want you. I could easily live without a baby as long as I have you." He pulled her close and held her while they stood in the kitchen. She had tears running down her cheeks.

Chapter 19

The rest of the week went by without incident. Leela had no dizzy spells and no black outs. She picked Ashley up for work every morning and took her home every night. Clay continued to meet her for lunch throughout the week, too. He even had flowers delivered to the diner for her on Wednesday after their discussion about babies the night before. By Friday Leela was anxious for the weekend. She was exhausted and afraid she was going to throw herself into her dizzy spells again, plus, Alex was coming up that weekend and they were going to stay at Clay's house with them. There was certainly enough room.

Clay and Leela went to the grocery store Friday night and bought enough groceries to feed an army. They bought breakfast foods, lunchmeats, dinner food, snacks, as well as vegetables and fruit. They also bought a deck of cards and a few new movies. Leela changed the sheets in the guest bedroom downstairs and put fresh flowers in a vase there. Clay was excited to be entertaining, and was looking forward to Saturday night as his sister and her husband were going to have dinner with them. Leela was nervous since she had never met her before but Clay assured her they'd get along great.

Leela had just started breakfast when Alex and Laura arrived on Saturday morning. They were grateful because they hadn't eaten before they left and just munched on some donuts on the way down. As they enjoyed breakfast they discussed their plans for the day.

Clay and his brother in law, Patricia's husband, were

the groomsmen, so Alex and Clay were going to go pick out the tuxedos, then they were going fishing. Leela, Laura and Patricia were going to go look at the reception hall and church and maybe buy some more decorations. They had no idea how long that would take them, but if there was time afterward the ladies find something to do. They were all going to dinner that night at a nice restaurant just outside of Palmside.

Shortly after they'd finished cleaning up breakfast, Patricia and her husband Ed knocked on the door. Clay let them in and brought them to the kitchen to meet his fiancée. Patricia was four years senior to Clay and they looked very much alike. They seemed to have a good relationship, and Leela was surprised it had taken Clay so long to introduce them.

Patricia hugged Leela and told her she was happy to meet her and that she'd heard so much from both Laura and Clay. Ed seemed nice enough, and he and Clay were close.

The men decided if they were going to catch any fish they'd better get headed to the tuxedo shop. Laura showed Patricia the bridesmaid dresses she and Leela had picked out in D.C. and she tried hers on. It fit her well, and both ladies looked great in them so Laura was pleased. They decided they had better get moving to the church while the priest was still there, so off they went.

After reserving the church and reception hall, the ladies hit several of the craft stores in and around Palmside. Before she knew it Patricia had a trunk full of decorations and Laura was thrilled. They had stopped at Leela's diner to have lunch and the weekend staff was glad to see her. She didn't know many of them but some of them worked during the week, too. Sammy just happened to be there too, so Leela introduced her to Laura and Patricia.

It was three o'clock before they finished all their wedding shopping. They knew the guys wouldn't be home till around six so they decided to go visit Patricia and

Clay's mother and introduce Leela. She was nervous since Clay wasn't there with her, but Patricia assured her it would be fine. Her mother already loved her just from what she had been told. Leela was surprised to find her future mother-in-law's home to be even larger than Clay's, and she was nearly shaking with nervousness.

Patricia led them through the house to the backyard, where she knew her mother would be gardening. When she saw the three women walk up, she got up from her flowers and hugged Patricia and Laura and took Leela's hand. She looked at her and smiled. Clay looked just like her.

"I am so happy to meet you, dear. My Clay has done well for himself this time," she said with a smile.

"It's nice to meet you, too, Mrs. Warner." The four of them sat at the table in the garden and talked. Laura talked about the upcoming wedding and Mrs. Warner asked Leela if she'd thought about hers. Leela told her what she'd like and the women all agreed it would be beautiful. As Leela was sitting in the backyard at The Warner home she realized it would be the perfect place for her wedding. She didn't say anything to them because she wanted to run it by Clay first. It was beautiful with the flower garden and the tall trees that would no doubt drop lots of fall leaves, as well as a lovely little pond. Leela thought it was perfect and would be large enough to have the reception too, considering she didn't think there would be many guests.

At five-thirty they said goodbye to Mrs. Warner and headed back to Clay's house to get ready for dinner. Laura was thrilled at the way Leela and Patricia got along, and Patricia was equally thrilled with the success of Leela meeting her mother. By the time they arrived back at Clay's house the three women were best friends.

The guys were back by then and everyone scurried around the house getting ready for the restaurant Clay had made reservations at. By seven-fifteen everyone was dressed and ready, looking fit enough for the pages of a fashion magazine. They all drove to Palino's in Patricia's van so they could all ride together. When they walked in the door several heads turned to look at the handsome bunch. The host seated them almost immediately and Alex ordered wine.

"We're celebrating two engagements," he told the waiter. Leela smiled, she was so glad to have her brother back - and to have all her new friends.

They chatted easily while waiting for dinner to arrive, And when it did it was better than they could have imagined. It was the nicest Italian restaurant in the area, and made this night out with new friends the perfect occasion.

After they had eaten the waiter asked if anyone wanted dessert and they all declined. The meal had been wonderful, with generous portions, and they were all simply stuffed.

"Let's go dancing at Marietta's," Clay said as they discussed how to spend the rest of the evening.

"That sounds fun to me," Alex said.

"Sure," Ed and Patricia said at the same time. They all got up, piled in the van, and headed toward Marietta's, which was back in Palmside. It was nine-thirty when they arrived, and the place was packed. There were people dancing everywhere, and even though it was a nice place it was nothing compared to Maxine's in D.C. They got a table and ordered some wine before heading out onto the dance floor. First Leela danced with Clay, then she danced with Alex while Laura danced with Clay. Then she danced with Ed while Clay danced with Patricia. They had so much fun that they didn't realize it was almost one in the morning and the place was thinning out.

"I am so worn out," Laura said to Alex as they walked back to their table.

"Me, too," Leela and Patricia said at the same time. They had lost track of time and were shocked when the waiter told them it was last call. They finished their bottle of wine and headed back to Clay's house in the van.

Since it was so late, Clay offered Ed and Patricia the other guest room and they accepted thankfully. They had all had quite a bit to drink and they didn't want to drive any more than they had to. When they got back to Clay's house they all sat in the living room talking about how much fun they'd had. Even though they were all worn out from dancing, none of them were yet ready for bed, so they played cards until Patricia announced she couldn't keep her eyes open. It was three-thirty in the when they all agreed it was time for bed. By the time Leela's head hit her pillow she was out. Clay just lay there staring at her until he finally dozed off. He fell asleep thinking how beautiful Leela was, and when he finally dreamed, it was of her.

It was ten o'clock before anyone got up, and Leela was the first, with Laura waking shortly after. They started breakfast and decided not to wake up the others until it was almost done. The smell of sausage and bacon permeated the house, and before they could wake anyone up the smell brought them alive and to the kitchen. "Good morning, sweetheart!" Clay said to Leela as he kissed her on the cheek. Alex was right behind him followed closely by Patricia and Ed. They all looked like a train had hit them from the night before but they all agreed it was worth it. By the time everyone was up breakfast was ready and on the table.

They all ate and talked about how much fun dancing had been.

"I haven't been dancing in years," Patricia confessed.

"I'd only been dancing once before, and that landed me in a Washington paper," Leela said, laughing. They'd all seen the article and teased her about it.

The ladies cleaned the kitchen after breakfast and the men sat in the backyard drinking coffee. By the time the ladies joined them they had decided to go golfing for a few hours. Alex and Laura weren't leaving till the next morning so they had the day to kill.

Since Laura didn't have any more wedding errands to run, she asked the girls if they wanted to go to the day spa. After the night they had, they all agreed it sounded like a great idea. Leela had never been to the spa. It wasn't something she ever spent her money on, but since she was giving up her apartment she could afford it this once. Plus, she knew if she didn't do it Clay would pay for it - and she didn't want that. They all agreed to meet back at three for a late lunch then went their separate ways.

The spa was very relaxing. Leela had her first professional massage, and a manicure and pedicure. She soaked in a hot tub, and they all sat in a sauna room. By the time the ladies left they were as relaxed as could be. They decided to stop at a deli and get sandwiches to bring home because they didn't feel like cooking. When they did get home the guys were glad of it, as they were starved.

After they ate, they relaxed in the backyard underneath a shade tree. They were going to have dinner together and then Patricia and Ed were going home. They only lived thirty minutes from Clay on the other side of town, however they wanted to be home early because they both had to work the next day.

They started grilling the steaks about five and dinner was ready by quarter till six. They all sat in the kitchen eating and enjoying their last meal together this trip. By eight o'clock Patricia and Ed were getting ready to leave and they hugged all of them.

"I am so glad we met, Leela. I am thrilled to have you as a friend and a sister."

Leela hugged her back. "I feel the same way." They promised to call each other, and they left. The remaining four didn't feel like doing anything else so they settled in the living room with a movie Clay and Leela had bought. By the time it was over they were ready for bed.

That night Leela made love to Clay and he felt like he had the world. He had been thrilled to hear Leela met his mother, even though he had wanted to be the one to introduce them. He was glad they had gotten along so well.

"Clay?" Leela asked as they lay in bed.

"Huh?" he asked, almost asleep.

"I've been thinking about our wedding." That woke Clay up. He was almost afraid she'd changed her mind again.

"What, babe?" he asked cautiously.

"I think I found the perfect place. It's exactly what I want." Clay leaned up on his elbow so he could look at her face, smiling at the dreamy look he found there.

"Where?" He was interested in what she had to say.

"Your mom's house. Her backyard. I bet it is beautiful in the fall, and it's definitely big enough for the reception, too." Clay was shocked. He hadn't even thought of that, but knew she was right. It was perfect for what Leela described she wanted.

"I think that is a great idea," he said, giving her a gentle kiss on the cheek. "I'll call her tomorrow." They fell asleep holding each other, both thinking about their upcoming wedding. It was going to be perfect.

Chapter 20

Monday morning Alex and Laura left reluctantly around seven o'clock, with Clay leaving for work shortly after. Leela had to go get her weekly blood work done and then pick Ashley up for work.

The lab-tech vampires were a lot friendlier today than they had been in the past.

"Ms. Jacobs, Dr. Risinger would like to schedule an appointment with you for next week to do a follow-up to your accident a few weeks ago. What day would be best and what time?" Leela thought about it.

"How about Friday, as late as you can." She was scheduled for four o'clock on Friday, so she could just take off work early.

When she got to the diner she cleared her appointment for the following week with Sammy, and being nearly two weeks away it was not a problem. In between tables Leela told Ashley about her weekend and meeting Clay's family, and the possibility of having the wedding at his mother's. Ashley asked her when they should start planning it and Leela wasn't sure.

She had been to several bridal shops in the last few weeks with Laura, but her wedding would be different. The wedding and reception would be at the same place - that is if Mrs. Warner agreed - which Clay assured Leela she would. The fall flowers would have to wait till then anyway. They did, however, decide to take a weekend soon and go look at dresses for both of them. Clay couldn't meet her for lunch today because he had a meeting with his boss about an upcoming project, so she and Ashley took their break together and they sat in the back room and ate.

"You look so happy, Leela. It's a complete one eighty from three months ago." Leela smiled.

"I know. I can barely believe it myself. Most of the time I think I'm dreaming." They only had thirty minutes but they had managed to talk about Ryan, too. He was having some problems in school with behavior and Ashley was sure it was stemming from the loose leash his father kept on him.

"He gets away with everything," Ashley complained to Leela before they had to go back to work.

Leela's landlord had agreed to let Leela break her lease early since there was only two and a half months left, so after she got off work she was going to her apartment to start packing and Clay was going to meet her there. It took them all week packing after work to finally clear out the apartment. By the weekend they were exhausted and decided to do nothing but relax. Their only plans were to visit his mother, so they could ask her about the wedding.

Saturday they sat in Mrs. Warner's backyard when Clay decided it was time. "Mom, did Leela tell you how she wanted our wedding in the fall?" His mother nodded. She thought it was a lovely idea.

"In October, is that right, dear?" she said to him.

"Yes, Mom. We wanted an outdoor wedding in a fall setting and last weekend when Leela was here she thought this might be the perfect place. We'd like to get married here, Mom. What do you think?" His mom jumped to her feet and hugged Leela.

"I think that's a perfect idea, dear. It's so beautiful here in the fall." Leela took a deep breath of relief. Clay was sure his mom would agree, but Leela had been nervous.

For the next hour they talked about the wedding and then they left to go home. Leela was thrilled - it was all coming together.

As they lay in bed that night Leela realized it had been almost three weeks since she'd had an episode. It was a miracle, she thought. Oddly enough Clay was lying next to her thinking the same thing. He was convinced miracles do happen.

They relaxed the rest of the weekend at the house. Leela unpacked most of her things and stored what she didn't need in his garage. She didn't need any of her pots and pans and towels and things like that. Clay had made a place for her clothes in the master room and gave her a closet in the hallway, too. She put her pictures up in the bedroom, but not anything else. Clay encouraged her to redecorate the house if she wanted to, but she didn't feel the need. She loved it the way it was and it didn't feel right changing a thing.

When Leela went to the clinic on Monday morning for her weekly blood draw, the nurse Paulina reminded her of her appointment on Friday. Clay begged Leela to let him go, and she finally relented. The week went by without an episode again and by Friday Leela was as nervous as could be about the appointment. Clay met her at the diner and they drove together in his car.

"Leela Jacobs?" Paulina called from the doorway that led back to the examination rooms. Leela and Clay stood up and followed Paulina back to the room. There she handed Leela a gown and asked her to put it on, and then told her they needed a urine sample as well. Leela was confused because they'd never asked her for that before, and her fears of getting worse began to creep in.

Ten minutes later, Dr. Risinger came into the room and Leela introduced Clay, telling the doctor they were planning on getting married in the fall. A sly smile crossed Dr. Risinger's face as he shook clay's hand.

"Leela, your blood tests for the last three weeks have been inconsistent with the months before." Leela wasn't sure what he meant by that. "How have you been feeling?" Clay looked as nervous as Leela did.

"I've felt fine actually. Better than ever. I haven't had a dizzy spell or blackout for over three weeks." The doctor smiled.

"I was hoping you'd say that, Leela, because your blood tests look increasingly better. As a matter of a fact the first week it looked better, we thought we had switched your blood with someone else's, and that is why we had you come back. When the next two week's tests came back the same, I realized there could be no mistake."

Leela was confused, Clay even more so. He had never heard of anyone getting better with her blood disorder. Only staying stable.

"What have you done differently in the last month that you hadn't done before?" the doctor asked.

"I've been happy?" Leela said shyly. She knew it was a stupid answer but there was no other answer.

"I guess that is it then," the doctor said.

"I don't understand," Clay said, confused.

"I'm sorry, what is your name again, sir?" the doctor asked Clay.

"Clay - Clay Warner."

Dr. Risinger beamed at him. "Nice to meet you, Clay. Looks like you were the right medicine for this young lady. She has reverted back to stage one, and her blood work is looking very normal."

Leela was shocked. She didn't know what to say.

"Is that possible- I - I didn't know that was even possible." The truth is the doctor had never seen a patient come close to remission, the most anyone could hope for was symptom control.

"Some things are unexplainable, Ms. Jacobs. This is just one of them." Clay was so happy he enfolded her in his arms and kissed her cheek.

"There is one other thing, though, Ms. Jacobs, and I am not completely sure I should inform you of this with Mr. Warner in the room."

Clay looked at Leela, almost hurt, but he asked,

"Would you like me to step out?"

Leela shook her head. "No, Dr. Risinger, no secrets here. It's okay."

Then Dr. Risinger smiled. "Leela, you're pregnant. Three weeks!" Leela's jaw dropped and Clay looked like someone had shot him.

What did he just say? "What?" Leela asked.

"Well, your blood test this week had elevated hormonal levels, so we ran a pregnancy test from your urine sample. It's positive." That wasn't the explanation she wanted, she had been told by Dr. Risinger four months ago she couldn't get pregnant. Her illness was supposed to make her barren, and now she was in near-remission and pregnant?

"But I thought you said I'd be sterile?" she asked, confused again.

"Another miracle?" he answered. There was no scientific explanation for it, the doctor was as puzzled as they were.

Leela looked at Clay as he had been silent since the doctor had dropped the pregnancy bombshell on them. He was staring at her in amazement. *Two miracles in one hour. Wow.*

"Leela, oh my God!" A huge smile covered Clay's face. Leela had tears in her eyes. It was what she dreamed of and never thought would come true.

"Ms. Jacobs, there is still a big risk of carrying a baby with this condition. Women who suffer from it and get pregnant have a high risk of miscarriage. You'll have to take it easy. The diner job may be okay for now, but as you progress you may have to take some time off. You're still a bit frail, Ms. Jacobs, and you have a lot against you."

Clay looked at Leela. "You can quit, Leela. I make more than enough money to support us." Leela looked at Clay, not sure what to say.

"We'll talk about that later."

The doctor started again. "We are going to continue

your weekly blood draws for the next three months. If they continue to stay as they are - and you are doing fine with your pregnancy - we will start doing them every two weeks. You'll see me once every two weeks, starting now, for checkups. And around six months we'll start weekly. You are at high risk and I want to make sure we come out of this with a baby." Leela nodded.

"Will my baby have what I have?" she asked, worried.

"Not necessarily. It's much like the more common hemophilia, but requires both parents to carry the gene for the chance of your baby having it." The doctor nodded toward clay, "As long as this young man doesn't have a family history of the disorder, your baby should be just fine."

As they left the doctor's office Leela was in shock and Clay was beaming.

"This is a dream come true, Leela, isn't it?" Leela looked at him and smiled. She was nervous, this was a lot to take in. She was not only getting better but having a baby, too?

"It is a dream, Clay. I cannot believe it's happening." She was in such a daze that Clay looked concerned.

"Leela, do you not want this?" he asked.

"I want this more than anything in the world, Clay. But I am scared to death of anything going wrong." Clay realized it was a valid fear.

They went straight home instead of going to the diner to get Leela's car. She suddenly felt vulnerable and Clay wanted to get her home. As they sat on the couch he held her while they tried to absorb what they had just been told.

Leela spoke up. "Clay, I want you to know that this is a miracle for me - for us. I am afraid to lose it. And if things go well I will be the happiest person on this earth. Until then I will be a nervous wreck. The first three months are the most common for miscarriage. I'd like to hold off telling anyone until we are past the three month stage." Clay realized she was right.

"If that's what you want, and I agree. I think it's a smart thing to do. Are you going to continue working?"

Leela thought about it for a minute. "Yes, as long as I can. I don't want to change things too much yet, and the doctor said I should be okay at first."

Clay nodded. He had figured she would say that. "I do want you to tell Ashley - so if anything happens at work she knows what is going on." Leela nodded. Ashley was her best friend. She'd love to tell her.

The rest of the weekend was a blur. They wanted to be happy for their news but they were too nervous. This was a blessing they never thought they'd get and now they were going to fight like hell to keep it. Sunday they decided to ask Ashley and Ryan over to tell her. When they did, Ashley jumped with glee. It was the first sign of celebration Clay had seen since they'd found out. It occurred to him they were treating it like a curse.

They quickly advised Ashley that she was the only one who'd know until the second trimester and she vowed to keep their secret, but after she promised she congratulated them, and for the first time since they found out Leela smiled about it and actually looked happy. Clay was relieved. He had silently questioned whether or not Leela really wanted to carry their child, but he knew this was a lot for her to absorb all at once. She was not only getting better and getting her life back, but she was getting a baby, too.

Chapter 21

Leela went to her normal blood draw on Monday morning as usual then picked up Ashley, who made a big deal to ask her how she felt. Leela said she was fine and reminded her of her promise to keep quiet about the pregnancy. Ashley promised once again and hugged her.

Monday was busy as normal and Leela worked just as hard to keep up with her tables. Leela had caught Ashley watching her several times throughout the day and knew that was why she didn't want anyone to know - people worry about her constantly, and that wasn't something she wanted. Clay sent her flowers that day and Leela was relieved when five o'clock finally rolled around. She thought it was odd that she didn't feel any different. She thought she should have.

When Leela arrived home Clay had dinner waiting on the table. They had a good evening alone talking.

"Boy or girl?" Clay asked her after they cleaned up after dinner.

"I don't know," she said honestly. She hadn't even thought about it. She was so overwhelmed by the news.

"I'm almost afraid to say. I don't want to jinx us." Clay smiled. "I'd love either. As long as the baby looks like you." She laughed. "God. I hope not." They talked about the baby a little while longer and then settled down to watch TV before bed.

The rest of the week flew by and Clay and Leela were having dinner at his mom's house with Patricia and Ed. It took all Clay had not to tell them. He wanted to share their news so bad but honored Leela's wishes not to. They had a good dinner.

Patricia and Ed were going to New York for a week and his mother asked Leela if she had any more plans for the wedding. Patricia had thought it was a brilliant idea to have the wedding there and promised to help Leela with whatever she needed. When they brought up the wedding Leela realized she would be five months pregnant at the time. She made a mental note to discuss it with Clay when they got home.

Saturday Leela and Clay went shopping and Clay insisted on buying a swing set for the backyard. Leela teased him that his child wouldn't be able to play on it for years and he said it was for Ryan, but Leela thought it was just an excuse for him. Clay had wanted to go into a furniture store and pick out furniture for the baby's room, but Leela told him they had to wait until the second trimester. He was disappointed but agreed. When they got home they ate lunch in the backyard and Leela remembered the wedding.

"Clay, I'll be five months pregnant when we get married in October. Are you sure you want to marry a pregnant woman?" she asked, teasing him.

"I think you'll make a beautiful pregnant woman and I'd love to marry you all big and fat." She laughed and kissed his forehead.

"Honestly, Clay, should we postpone it?" Clay thought for a minute.

"What do you want, Leela? I would love nothing more than to marry you with child. I think you're beautiful now and I think you'll be twice as beautiful then. But I want the wedding to be everything you've dreamed of and want. We can get married now, or we can wait until afterward. It won't be a fall wedding, though. Or we can just stick to our original plan." Leela thought about it for a minute.

"I don't want to get married now. We are still trying to get Alex and Laura married. And I'd hate to wait. I am okay with being pregnant." Clay smiled.

"Then October it is."

Clay and Leela relaxed the rest of the weekend and the following week Leela felt a bit weak, but nothing that she was overly concerned about. She was four weeks pregnant and was starting to get used to the idea. Clay had started buying healthier food and Leela had a bigger appetite than she usually did. She still went for her weekly blood draw and at week six she went to the doctor for her first pregnancy checkup.

"Hello, Leela. How have you been feeling lately?" Dr. Risinger asked.

"I've been fine. I get weak sometimes but no spells or episodes like before. I am still working and think I will be okay to continue for now." Dr. Risinger nodded. He was very happy with Leela's blood work the last few weeks as she had much improved. She was not in remission, but still holding firmly in stage one. All the symptoms for stage two were gone.

"Let's check for a heart beat," he said as he put something that looked like a little recorder on her flat stomach, and suddenly she heard a small thumping sound.

"Sounds great, Leela." She thought it was too fast to be a heartbeat but the doctor explained to her that it would be fast for quite some time. "I'd like to do an ultrasound as well." He showed her back to the radiology and laid her on a table.

"Here's our little miracle," he said as he found the fetus. "Looks great. Would you like pictures to show your fiancé?" Leela nodded yes and Dr. Risinger printed several pictures for her. It was amazing. Leela couldn't believe her baby was on the screen in front of her - it was a miracle.

When Leela got home from her appointment Clay was already home sitting in the backyard.

"Look, honey," she said as she handed Clay the ultrasound photos.

"Is this our baby?" he asked. She was so excited about

the doctor's appointment that she hadn't noticed he was a bit preoccupied.

"Yes, isn't the baby perfect?" she said, mesmerized by the photo.

"Just perfect," Clay replied. He had some news to tell her but that wasn't the time.

They had dinner and settled down to watch TV when Leela realized Clay was being unusually quiet.

"Babe, what's wrong?" Clay took a deep breath. If he was going to tell her, now was as good a time as any.

"Leela, they asked me to go work in Texas to set up a hospital. I told my boss no but he isn't too happy about it. If they don't find someone else to do it by the end of June I'm going to have to." Leela looked crushed, nearly as crushed as she felt when he had to go to Washington. This was Texas, even farther away.

"Do you think you'll have to go? What about Alex and Laura's wedding? What about our wedding and the baby? What about me?" Clay had known she wouldn't take it well.

"Leela, baby, this is my job and I already made a stink about D.C. I may get out of the Texas job but what about the next one. If I don't want to do the traveling I may just have to find a new job." Leela didn't know what to say. This wasn't at all what she wanted but she refused to break down like she did the last time. He was right.

"Well, I guess you'll just have to do what you have to do then," she said half-heartedly. He knew she was hurt but he didn't know what else to do.

"Want to watch a movie?" Leela asked as if nothing had happened and Clay was confused by her subject change.

"Leela, don't you think we should talk about this?" Leela looked at him and smiled.

"Now, honey, what is there to talk about? You'll try to get someone else to do the job. If you can't, then you'll go. I have no say in this so there is nothing left for me to talk about." She turned on the TV.

Clay was upset that she was acting like this but he didn't want to show her. He knew that she was hurting and trying not to show it, but when they went to bed that night he heard her crying softly. He just put his arms around her and hugged her; there was nothing else he could do.

The next two weeks Leela walked around like a zombie. Clay could see she was no longer happy and he knew it was because of his work. He still had two weeks to get a replacement and he was searching as hard as he could to find one. There was another possibility - a job promotion that would allow him to travel less. He had applied for it shortly after telling Leela he may have to go to Texas and wouldn't know more until it would be nearly time to leave Clay felt like he had a shot at the job even though two of his fellow employees had applied.

Clay was worried about Leela and more than once called Ashley to make sure she was doing okay at work. Ashley told him she was doing fine, and that didn't help any.

Ashley was aware of the strain Leela had been under but Leela hadn't told her why. Nobody knew that Clay might be going to Texas for an indefinite amount of time. By the end of June Leela was visibly worn out, she was ten weeks pregnant by then and was starting to get a little pouch in her belly. She was almost out of her danger zone and they were two weeks from announcing their good news to the world. Leela just hoped Clay would be around to tell everyone with her.

On the last day of June when Clay was preparing what he would say to Leela when he had to leave for Texas, he got called into his boss' office. He nearly hugged his supervisor when he told Clay he had gotten the promotion to lead computer programmer. Not only did it mean more money to spoil their baby with, it meant not having to leave Leela - now or ever - on long assignments. He may have to travel for a week at a time for meetings and conferences in the future, but nothing long -term. When he called Leela to tell her after he had left the office she was ecstatic. It had been a long four weeks worrying about him leaving, and now it was finally over.

Two weeks after Clay's promotion, and with only another two weeks left before her brother's wedding, Leela called Alex and told him the good news. Alex was so shocked he thought he'd heard her wrong, and when he realized she was three months pregnant he was she had kept the news from him.

"Nobody knew, Alex. I was so much at risk we thought it would be easier not to tell anyone until it was safe." Alex understood but was still hurt. He asked Leela about the wedding and she told him she was continuing as planned. When Laura got on the phone she was so happy for Leela she cried.

"I am so thrilled, Leela," and Leela started crying tears of joy, too.

Leela assured Laura that her dress still fit and most likely would by the time of her wedding, and Laura told her not to be silly, if it didn't fit they'd have it altered. By the time they said goodbye they were all in good spirits. Alex thanked God for his sister's good fortune.

Next Clay called his sister and Ed and got the same reaction from them. Shocked and then thrilled. His mother was thrilled as well. She was afraid it would affect the wedding plans but Leela assured her it wouldn't. The next day at the diner she told everyone there. Sammy, who was bulging at the belly, congratulated her and promised her some of her maternity clothes she could no longer wear. By the end of the twelfth week of Leela's pregnancy everyone she knew was had been told she was having a baby, and no one was happier than Leela and Clay.

The next two weeks went by quickly, and before they knew it they were getting ready for Alex and Laura's wedding. It was two days away and time was flying.

Chapter 22

The day before the wedding Laura, Leela, and Patricia were busy getting every detail ready for the wedding. Laura was nervous, not about marrying Alex, she loved him and wanted to spend the rest of her life with him. She was afraid something would go wrong.

When the time came, everything was perfect. Leela thought Laura was the most beautiful bride and when she told Clay he said possibly, but only because her turn wasn't for three months. After a minor alteration Leela's dress fit her perfectly. The whole wedding was beautiful, with Laura in a long and flowing gown that had a yard-long train. Alex looked so handsome it brought tears to her eyes, and she thought lovingly of their parents.

They would have been so proud of him. He had a great job - and now a lovely wife. The wedding was more beautiful than anyone could have imagined. The reception was immediately after the ceremony, and they had a live band and catered food. There was close to one hundred people there, most of which Leela didn't know. Leela met a lot of Laura's family as well as some of their childhood friends, and most of them knew Clay. Alex had some coworkers and friends from Virginia there, too. Leela had noticed that Alex hadn't invited anyone from back home in Indiana, realizing that was just part of his life he wanted to forget.

They all danced and mingled until ten o'clock, and Leela was exhausted. She wasn't drinking due to her pregnancy and she made sure to take frequent breaks from being on her feet. Clay had made sure everyone there knew that Leela was his fiancée, they were getting married in three months, and that she was having his baby. Leela felt like a prize horse Clay was showing off, but she was happy that he felt she was good enough to show. Leela still didn't feel she was beautiful enough to enjoy clay's attentions.

Leela made a mental note of several of the people he was close to so she could make they were invited to their wedding.

"Can I have the last dance, sis?" Alex said as he walked up to where she was sitting.

"Of course," she said as she stood up to dance with him. They glided around the dance floor easily.

"I'm happy for you," Alex said to her.

"Well, big brother, I'm happy for you," she said back, smiling at him.

"You deserve a happy life, Lee, and Clay is a great guy. I want you to be happy. I want you to be healthy, too, so please, make sure you take care of yourself." She blushed.

"Alex, I'm happy, and I promise to take care of myself. I am getting better." Alex had been thrilled about that. He was still not sure how it was possible, but he was glad it happened. They spent the rest of their dance chatting about how great the day had been, and by the time the song had ended they stood there hugging each other. Leela was so glad he'd come back into her life.

The band had ended their final set and started packing up. Leela, Laura and Patricia were walking around cleaning up when Leela felt a sharp pain in her stomach. It was so sharp that she couldn't stand up straight, and all she could do was bend over, clutching her stomach. Clay had been watching her from across the room admiring her, when he saw her double over, and he came running.

"Leela? Are you okay?" When he said that the others came to her, too. Leela didn't know what was happening. The pain had yet to stop and she couldn't move.

"Leela, what is it, baby?" Clay asked, immediately

panicked.

"My stomach - sharp pain - can't move," was all she could get out. She wasn't sure, but she thought she might have been bleeding also. She tried to tell Clay but before she could say a thing she fainted.

Clay caught her before she hit the ground, but didn't know what to do. "Someone call 911!" he said frantically. Patricia ran to the table where her purse was, pulled out her cell phone and dialed 911.

She told the operator that Leela had passed out and she was pregnant and very sick. When she looked back over toward Leela she saw that there was a puddle of blood underneath her and Clay was crying. Patricia knew that it couldn't be good, and was afraid Leela might be having a miscarriage. By the look of Alex and Laura they had the same thought.

Alex was leaned over his sister who was being held by her fiancé. Laura looked at Patricia and without saying a word to each other, they both knew what the other thought. Neither of them thought it was fair, Not to Clay, and not to Leela.

It took the ambulance five minutes to get there, and by the time they arrived Leela was sobbing and covered in blood. Clay looked like he was in shock and just kept saying over and over to Leela that it would be okay. He hadn't let go of her since she fainted.

The paramedics laid Leela on the gurney and Clay stayed by her side holding her hands. After slamming the doors on the back of the ambulance, the paramedics told both Alex and Laura they would do everything they could, but the looks on their face told the newlyweds that Leela would likely lose the baby. The ambulance drove away with the sirens blaring.

Alex grabbed Laura and held her. He couldn't believe this was happening - especially on their wedding day. He wanted happy memories, not sad ones, on this day.

"Let's get to the hospital," Alex said to Laura. Patricia

and Ed promised to finish cleaning up and then meet them there.

Alex and Laura stopped by Clay's house on the way to the hospital to change and grab a change of clothes for Clay and Leela, too. Thirty minutes later they were in the emergency room asking after Leela.

"She's been taken to surgery; you can find Mr. Warner in the second floor waiting room," the receptionist told them. Alex looked horrified when she said surgery, knowing most likely that would mean a D&C procedure. The walked in silence to the elevator and rode up to the second floor, and when they stepped out they found clay crying alone in a dark corner.

"She lost the baby," he said through his sobs. Laura leaned down and hugged him.

"I'm so sorry, Clay. Is she okay?" Clay shook his head.

"I don't know. They said she lost too much blood so they had to give her transfusions, and then they had to - had to take the baby. She was passed out when we got here. I'm not even sure she knows yet." He looked up at Alex with red eyes.

"I'm so sorry, Alex. This isn't the way I wanted you to remember your wedding day." Alex hugged Clay and told him it wasn't his fault and they couldn't help it. Alex was wracked with guilt because he had made Leela dance with him right before it happened.

It was an hour later when the doctor came out to the waiting room and told them she was in recovery. She would be there for an hour and then they could see her. He told them that she would be okay after they gave her some blood. Clay asked if there was any damage, and the doctor - understanding his question - told clay she could still bear children, although she would still be at high risk due to her disease. He told them to go to the fourth floor waiting room and he'd come get them when she got to her room.

Clay told Alex and Laura to go back to the hotel and

salvage what they could of their wedding night, but they wouldn't have anything to do with it. They were leaving the next afternoon for their honeymoon, and until then they wanted to be there for Leela and Clay. They knew once they saw Leela they wouldn't stay long, it was after midnight and they knew she'd need her rest. When the doctor finally came to tell them she was settled in, Clay was pacing the room.

"You three can go see her now, but I must warn you. She is very upset. We just told her about the baby and she didn't take it well. She did say it was okay for you to see her, though. She is going to be in the hospital for a few days so we can monitor her and her blood levels. Her condition may be affected by the miscarriage so they need to make sure it doesn't get out of hand.

Clay wasn't prepared for what he saw when he walked into the hospital room, Leela was crying and very pale. She had an IV in one arm with fluids and an IV with blood going into the other. She looked so sad no one knew what to say to her.

"Leela, oh baby, are you okay?" Clay said as he rushed to her side and hugged her. It only made the tears flow harder and she couldn't answer him. Laura and Alex were crying, too. She didn't deserve this.

After Leela finally calmed down, they all sat there in silence. Alex and Laura realized it probably wasn't best for them to be there, so they hugged her goodbye and promised to come see her the next morning. Leela felt awful and didn't really want company, but hadn't wanted to tell them to leave, either.

When they were alone Leela looked at Clay with tears in her eyes. "I'm so sorry," was all she could say.

"Oh, honey, it's okay. It's not your fault. You couldn't have done anything to change this."

Leela shook her head.

"Yes, I could have. I overdid it today. It's my fault, Clay. It's my damn sickness. I knew better than to be that active. It's all my fault." She cried over and over again. Clay knew that no matter how many times he assured her it wasn't her fault she wouldn't accept it, so he just hugged her tight and told her he loved her. It was almost morning by the time she finally fell asleep. Clay, however, didn't. He just sat there crying in the dark, thinking about the baby they'd never have.

Chapter 23

Clay woke up at seven A.M. Sunday morning in the same hospital chair he had fallen asleep in. Leela was still asleep. They had given her something to help her sleep and it was working. They had offered Clay a sleep aid - and a pullout bed - but he had declined.

At eight o'clock Patricia and Ed walked in. Patricia hugged Clay as he told her they'd lost the baby. Patricia had talked to Laura the night before and knew all the details, and felt so horrible for them. Clay told them that Leela wasn't doing so well, and that it was probably best if they came back later after she woke up, and they understood. They had contemplated coming at all, but Patricia had to see her brother. She could see that this had taken a toll on him.

Leela woke up a half-hour after Patricia and Ed left, and she refused to eat anything. She wasn't saying much and Clay was worried about her. He knew that this was hard on her and feared she would fall into a depression. The doctor had told her it was always a risk when a woman, even healthy, has a miscarriage. Clay had tried to start many conversations with her, but she refused to say any more than a few words.

Alex and Laura arrived around noon. Their flight was leaving at three and they had to be at the airport by two. They knew from Patricia that Leela hadn't been doing well and probably wasn't up for company, but Alex refused to leave until he saw her. Leela gave a weak smile at Alex when he walked in. Alex wanted a minute alone with his sister, so Clay and Laura decided to walk out and get some fresh air. It was the first time he had left Leela's side.

"Alex, I'm sorry about ruining your wedding day," Leela said, starting to cry again.

"Leela, don't, you didn't ruin anything. I'm sorry this happened." He didn't know what else to say. He just wanted to be there for her and didn't know how.

"I love you, Leela," Alex said with tears in his eyes.

"I love you, too," she said, crying even harder. Alex hugged her and they sat there holding each other for a long time. Both of them knew there was nothing either of them could say to make it better.

"I'm supposed to leave today for Paris. But if you want - I'll stay." he said to her when she finally pulled away.

"No, Alex, go and have fun. I'll be home in a few days anyway." He had abandoned her after they lost their parents, and he refused to do that to his sister again. Laura had already told him if he felt he needed to stay she was okay with postponing the honeymoon. In the end Leela wouldn't have let him stay anyway, she already felt like she ruined his wedding day and wasn't going to let him skip his honeymoon, too.

Thirty minutes later Laura and Clay walked back in, Clay had called Ashley while out of the room and filled her in on what happened. She had started crying on the phone, which brought tears back to clay's eyes. He was shocked he had any tears left.

When he came back into the room Leela didn't look any better. She looked drained and she hadn't been up very long. Alex tried to get her to eat something since Clay hadn't had any luck, and she once again refused. The doctor said that if she wouldn't eat he would have to order a feeding tube, but that didn't motivate her any, either. At one-thirty Laura and Alex hugged Leela and Clay goodbye and promised to call. They'd be back in a week and would be returning to Palmside for one final weekend before heading home.

The rest of the day didn't go any better and all Leela did was sleep. She hadn't even wanted to talk to Clay. He felt like there was nothing he could do for her so he stopped trying to make conversation, but she let him hold her most of the day. When her dinner tray came that night Clay begged her to eat. She thought he looked pathetic so decided to give it a try. She sat up in bed and that seemed to take tremendous energy for her. She picked at her chicken and her applesauce, but she did drink all her sweet tea. Clay had a tray delivered, too, with the same thing, and much to his surprise he couldn't eat that much either. The nurse was happy for her effort and told her so.

That night the nurse gave her something to help her sleep again and when offered, Clay graciously accepted. He was exhausted and knew he couldn't sleep on his own. He had already called his boss at work and they had told him to take the week off. He wouldn't have gone in anyway so he was thankful for their understanding.

Monday morning Dr. Risinger walked into Leela's hospital room. He was disappointed to see this happen to her as she had been doing so well. Much to his disappointment her blood tests showed her condition had regressed. Leela's condition was once again getting worse. He didn't want to deliver such a blow to her when she was already so down about the baby, but he had no choice.

"Leela, I hate to tell you this, but your condition is getting worse. It looks like the miscarriage pushed you back into stage two." She didn't say anything to him, just nodded. What could she say? Her life was falling apart. She was to the point where she didn't care. Clay had wanted to cry but knew he needed to be strong for her.

"Leela, you got better once. I'm convinced you can do it again. You can even try for another baby." Leela didn't respond. She had no plans to get pregnant again. This had been nearly impossible to deal with once and a second time would kill her.

When Dr. Risinger left the room, Clay took Leela's

hand. Much to his surprise she pulled away.

"I'm sorry, Clay, I just don't feel like being touched." Clay didn't know what to say. He was hurt but tried not to let her see. "I think you should go home tonight," she said next.

"No, Leela, I'm staying with you," he said firmly. She could stop him from touching her but he wouldn't leave. Leela looked him straight in the eye.

"Clay, I love you, but I'd like to be alone for a little while." Clay was about to object before realizing she hadn't been alone since it happened.

"Okay, I'm going to go home, change clothes, and get a few things. I'll be back in a little while." Leela gave him a small smile.

"Thanks," was all she said.

Clay left his cell number with the nurse and walked out to his car. When he sat down in it he put his head on the steering wheel and started to sob. He couldn't believe this was happening - first the baby, and now her condition getting worse again. He was so angry this was happening to her that he started pounding on the steering wheel, crying harder with every blow. It was ten minutes before he was able to pull out of his parking spot.

When he finally drove out of the parking lot he didn't know where to go. He didn't even remember driving there but a few minutes later pulled into his driveway. After letting himself in he sat down on the couch and stared at the wall. He wasn't sure if Leela would ever come out of this - the baby had been their dream, their miracle. Now it was gone. Leela was in a deep depression he couldn't bring her out of and wasn't sure life would ever be the same.

He finally found his way to the shower and spent a long time underneath the hot spray. An hour later when he got out the phone was ringing. It was Alex; the hospital had told him that Clay had gone home for a while.

"How is she?" he asked sadly.

"I don't know what to do," Clay said, starting to cry.

"She made me leave her, she said she had to be alone. Alex, I..." Clay started sobbing. Alex felt horrible. He wanted to get on a plane and come straight home but Clay told him that Leela wouldn't want that. Clay told Alex about the condition and how it had gotten worse again, then told him about the depression Leela had sunk into. Alex could barely stand what was happening to his sister. If Clay was this upset Leela had to be much worse, Clay always seemed to hold it together for her. Clay told him he had to get back to the hospital and would call him the next day. Reluctantly Alex hung up and reported what he had discovered to Laura, who felt just as guilty for not being there.

Clay got back to the hospital in time for dinner. He saw flowers on the nightstand and when he looked they were from Sammy and Ashley. Leela was sleeping in her bed and the nurse told him she'd slept most of the day. He asked the nurse if he should be worried and was told that if Leela didn't come out of the depression on her the doctors may have to resort to antidepressants.

Clay eased down beside Leela on the small hospital bed, wrapping her in an embrace. "I love you, Leela!" he whispered in her ear before he closed his eyes and fell asleep.

Chapter 24

Leela woke up and realized Clay was in her bed with her. It was dark outside and she knew it must be night. She had lost track of herself, and was unsure of even what day it was. She felt like she had been living in a nightmare.

She lay there looking at Clay wondering why he loved her so much, she seemed to radiate bad luck, first the baby, and now the condition. The doctor had been very blunt with her while Clay was gone, telling her if the depression wasn't put in check it could exacerbate her blood disorder. Leela didn't want her condition to deteriorate, but couldn't help feeling depressed after losing the baby.

Even though she didn't feel better, she made a conscious decision to *try* to get better -If not for herself, for Clay. She felt that she owed him so much after losing his baby. She leaned over and kissed his cheek. He looked so peaceful lying there. She knew it had been hard on him, too. She saw him crying when he thought she wasn't looking, or when he thought she was asleep. The truth was she had lost herself, but she was ready to try for him.

Clay started to wake up, and when he saw her smiling at him he smiled back.

"Hi," he said, not sure what else to say.

"Hi, baby." She wanted to say so much but knew it wouldn't come out right. "I'm a bit hungry. Could you tell the nurse to bring us some food?"

He jumped right out of bed. It was like she finally woke up. He kissed her on the forehead and ran to the nurses' station. They saw him coming and at first thought something was wrong.

"Mr. Warner, is everything okay?"

Clay almost laughed.

"She is hungry. Can we get her some food?" The nurse smiled at him.

"That is great. I'll get her a tray right now." She nodded at him and he knew she was telling him everything would be okay, and for the first time since they'd been there he thought it just might be.

Leela shocked Clay by eating all the dinner the nurse had sent her. She even attempted to start a conversation, although she was unsure about what to say. In the end they ended up talking about Laura and Alex and what a great time they were having in Paris. Clay knew they were worried, too, so he promised himself he'd call them later. Leela was still a little groggy from the medicine they had been giving her and she asked the nurse if they could cut it back a bit because she didn't want to sleep all the time. The nurse said she'd run it by the doctor but didn't see a problem with it. Later that night Clay went to the hall and called Alex, but they were out so he left a message at their hotel, letting them know Leela was better, not to worry. He hoped that would be enough to ease their minds. Little did he know that in Paris they were discussing coming home early. Neither of them could enjoy themselves with what was going on back home.

That night Leela and Clay stayed up till almost midnight talking and watching TV. Clay knew that she was coming out of it, but wasn't sure why. It really didn't matter, though; as long as she got better he'd be happy. When they did fall asleep that night he dreamed of their wedding. He hoped the miscarriage wouldn't postpone it.

Tuesday the doctor told Leela that if she did okay that day and night she could go home Wednesday morning, and Leela was glad to hear it. She was eager to get to her own bed. She made it a point to eat enough to prove she was getting better. By Wednesday morning she was getting dressed in her own clothes, waiting for Clay to pull the car up.

Laura and Alex had been relieved to hear she was doing better on Monday night and even happier to hear she was going home, so they decided to stay in Paris. They promised her they'd see her Saturday afternoon.

When Leela got home she didn't know what to do. Clay suggested they take it easy and watch some TV on the couch, but Leela told him she'd had enough of being indoors after the cramped hospital room. In the end she decided she wanted to sit in the backyard. It was the end of July, and even though the sun was hot, it was beautiful underneath their shade tree.

They spent the day outside enjoying the sun. Clay had made lunch and brought it out on a tray for her, and although she still wasn't very hungry she made an effort to eat anyway. Clay knew that he couldn't expect an immediate recovery and was happy for the effort she gave.

The nights were still hard on her. She would lie in bed and think about the baby until the tears began to flow. Clay would hear her and put his arms around her, never having to ask what was wrong. It was obvious, and he had his moments as well, but concentrated all his energy on getting her better. The week flew by, and before they knew it Alex and Laura were back from Paris.

When they got to Clay's house where they were staying until Monday, Alex was shocked at how thin and pale Leela had become in such a short time. He was worried about her even though Clay assured him she was making progress.

While the guys unloaded the car Laura and Leela sat in the backyard under what had become Leela's favorite shade tree. She had sat there most of her days since she got home from the hospital.

"How was Paris?" Leela asked, trying to break the uncomfortable silence.

"It was nice. We saw a lot of sights," Laura said. She wanted to tell Leela that it would be okay and that she'd get pregnant again, but honestly didn't know if Leela would want to hear it.

Leela laughed. "You sound *sooo* excited. Are you sure you didn't spend the week in the hospital with me instead."

Laura gave a shy smile. "I'm so damn sorry about what happened, Leela. I was so worried about you." She had tears in her eyes as she said it.

Leela suddenly felt like she could open up to Laura. "I'm sorry, too. I feel so guilty and like a failure. I know it wasn't my fault but I can't shake the feeling. Clay is so worried about me that I make such an effort to make life normal again, but the truth is, Laura, I feel like shit. I can't stop feeling that way." Laura looked at Leela. She hadn't expected Leela to be so honest, but was glad she had been.

"I know, Leela. If you ever need to talk to someone other than Clay, feel free to call me at any hour. Please. I'm your sister now," she said with tears in her eyes as the two women hugged.

Clay and Alex were about to go out back when they saw the women hugging. "Let's give them a minute," Clay said. "She really hasn't opened up to me much about losing the baby." Alex nodded and sat back down at the kitchen table.

Alex and Clay grilled out steaks that night and Laura made salad and sides. Leela was feeling a bit weak so she sat in the kitchen and kept Laura company. Laura saw the effort Leela was making but knew it wasn't for herself. She was well aware that it was an act she was putting on for Clay. She told Alex as much when they went to bed that night.

"She's far from okay, Alex," Laura told him. Alex had that suspicion throughout the day as well.

Sunday morning Leela woke ahead of everyone else and was in the kitchen drinking some coffee when Alex walked in, stretching.

"Hey, sis. Sleep well?" Leela hadn't, but didn't tell him so.

"Yeah, how about you? I think that mattress needs to be replaced." Alex smiled at her.

"Leela, are you okay? And I don't just mean going with the flow of things. I know you're not going to be happy so soon but are you even on that path?" Leela could see what her brother was trying to say. She couldn't lie to him.

"No, Alex. I'm not even close to it. I've tried but I just can't be. I feel guilty and robbed. I feel like I was just given a death sentence. With all that, happy isn't really the feeling I get." Alex looked at her.

"Leela, I don't really know what to say. I won't say it will be okay because only you can make that happen. You have nothing to feel guilty about. It wasn't your fault. And to be honest I felt guilty, too. It was, after all, my reception you overdid it at." Leela looked horrified.

"Alex, don't feel guilty. It isn't your fault at all. Deep down I know it isn't mine either. I've thought about going to a support group that Dr. Risinger suggested. What do you think?"

Alex thought for a moment. He really disliked the idea of his sister needing to attend a support group, but thought maybe that was what she needed.

"If you think it would help, go for it." Alex walked over to Leela and hugged her. He had missed her so much.

An hour later Clay and Laura had gotten up. Laura and Alex were going to visit her family that afternoon and then come back for the evening. They were thinking about going out for dinner but had decided to wait to see if they felt like it. Leela knew that they really meant if she felt like it. By noon Leela and Clay were alone again.

"Want to go to the deli for lunch today?" Leela asked Clay. Clay was surprised because Leela hadn't much felt like leaving the house since they had been home.

"Sure, baby. Getting your appetite back?" he said

teasingly. Leela smiled at him. Her talk with Alex this morning made her feel better and she decided to try harder for Clay. No, not just for Clay. For herself, too.

Lunch was uneventful, and after eating they sat at the booth in the deli, subdued and quiet.

Leela finally broke the silence. "I think we should send out our invitations for the wedding next week."

Clay was thrilled to hear her say that. In the week she'd been home she hadn't mentioned the wedding once, and he had been afraid to bring it up with all the emotions cycling through her.

"Leela, I think that is a great idea. Do you want to go look at some today?" He was hoping she'd say yes, and was delighted when she did. They walked the two blocks to the bridal shop. Clay thought they should have driven but Leela insisted they walk, and she was winded by the time they got there.

"Let's sit down here and rest a minute," he said to her, and she nodded, grateful for the rest.

While in there they found several designs they liked, and in the end they decided on lacy white paper with silver script. She also picked out her veil, their unity candles - and with Clay's urging - looked at the wedding dresses, although she didn't really like any of them. Clay carried the candles and told the shopkeeper they would be back in the next couple days with their list of guests for the printings.

Leela seemed in good spirits as they walked back to the car, and Clay was surprised and thrilled she was in such a good mood. Leela had even surprised herself a bit. They headed back home and Leela sat down immediately and started to make a list of people. They had figured on no more than one hundred guests. It was, after all, at his mother's house. Leela didn't have many people to invite, so she invited everyone from the diner, Alex and Laura, and a few others, coming up with a total of twenty. Clay had started his list of coworkers and friends, and it came to almost fifty people. Then he started his family list, which shockingly came to almost thirty people, and before they knew it they had completed their list of guests. After everyone was accounted for they had a total of one hundred and ten.

Later in the afternoon Leela decided to take a nap, explaining to Clay she wanted to go out to dinner that night and wanted to make sure she was rested. He completely understood and decided to catch up on some of his work in his office at home.

Chapter 25

Leela's nap had done her some good. After waking up she took a shower and was dressed by the time Alex and Laura got home, and Laura noticed Leela looked much more relaxed. By six o'clock they were driving to the steak house.

Dinner was delicious and everyone was in good spirits as they ate. "We finished our wedding guest list today," Leela announced. "The invitations should go out by the end of next week." Clay grinned happily as she said that. He had told Alex the day before he was afraid Leela would back out, and everyone looked relieved now that she hadn't.

"That's great!" Laura said.

"Hopefully we'll get one." Alex joked and everyone laughed.

"You, Ashley, and Patricia are my bridesmaids, so we need to pick out what color the dresses should be. What'd you think?" Leela asked Laura.

The wedding colors were fall colors - orange, red, yellow, and brown.

"Maybe burnt orange? Or copper?" Laura suggested. Leela nodded, that didn't sound bad.

"We should go to D.C. one weekend to go to that store we went to last time," Laura announced. Leela nodded. It was a thought.

They were all disappointed when it was time to head back to the house. They sat up till late talking because Laura and Alex would be leaving the next day. It would be a few weeks before she could see them again, as they had a lot of work to catch up on after taking a week and a half off for the wedding and honeymoon.

Monday morning Alex and Laura left and Clay went to work, so Leela was found herself alone. She would be going to the doctor that afternoon but had the morning to rest after the exhausting weekend. Suddenly alone, Leela started to feel the anxiety of the last week rushing back to her. Without her family to keep her busy, all she could think about was the baby she'd lost.

Sitting alone in her room she cried herself to sleep, not waking again until noon. She got up and had a shower. then sat in the backyard under the shade tree. She had never told Clay but she was already decided on names for the baby she had just lost. She would have named the baby Clayton Marcus if it had been a boy, and Leigh Anne for a girl. The boy's name was after Clay, of course, and her father. And her mother's name had been Leigh Anne. Now she didn't have to worry about that, she was sure she would never get pregnant again. The doctor told her in the hospital it was possible but if her condition was again deteriorating, it would mean becoming truly barren. She'd cheated fate once and was sure she wouldn't get a second chance.

By two o'clock Leela was sitting in the waiting room at Dr. Risinger's office. As usual she first went for the blood draw before Paulina called her back to a room. Dr. Risinger commented on how good she looked, and Leela assumed he was just being nice. The doctor took her blood pressure and palpated her abdomen before telling her all looked well, and then he pulled out her blood results.

"Well, no change from last week, which isn't necessarily bad. You're not getting worse. How do you feel? Any blackouts?" Leela shook her head.

"No, nothing like that. I get tired after most activities and I'm getting depressed a lot." He knew she would, as most women do after such an ordeal. And her ordeal was worse with the condition involved.

He nodded at her. "I can give you something for the depression, Leela. A lot of women need it after miscarriages. It can only be a temporary thing, not something you have to depend on. It can just help you get through this tough time."

Leela thought about it and nodded. She'd let him give her the prescription and then talk to Clay about it later. An hour later she left the doctor's office with antidepressants and no good news.

That night Clay brought home take-out and they ate in the living room in front of the TV. Clay had asked how her appointment went and Leela told him about the depression medication. He wasn't sure what to say, so told her that if she thought it would make her feel better, then to try it. Leela decided she would.

The next two weeks flew by. Leela still wasn't working but had most of her energy back. She had gotten the wedding invitations mailed out and went shopping for a lot of the decorations. She had lunch with Ashley several times and they had dinner with Clay and Ryan a couple of times, too. Leela thought the medication seemed to be helping, and by the last weekend in August Leela felt well enough for a road trip.

Leela, Ashley, and Patricia drove to Virginia and picked up Laura, and the four of them drove to Washington to go dress shopping. Ed and Clay decided to go on a weekend fishing trip since the girls would be gone. Clay was worried about Leela but knew that his sister and the other ladies would take good care of her.

The four women got to D.C. by one o'clock and checked into their hotel suite that clay had reserved for them. It had two bedrooms with two twin beds in each, and they loved it. The ladies decided to go shopping immediately and get it out of the way, so they could enjoy themselves the rest of the day. They weren't going home until the next evening.

Everyone loved the little shop Leela had found on her first trip called The Perfect Fit. The ladies all bought a few dresses for themselves and then Leela found the perfect bridesmaid dresses. They were long and straight in a deep red color and reminded Leela of the color of oak leaves in autumn, and had wrist length sleeves. Leela didn't want to get anything sleeveless in case it was chilly the day of the wedding. All four girls loved them, and they found one to fit each of the bridesmaids.

After leaving the shop Laura talked Leela into finding her wedding dress in D.C., too. All the dresses sent back to the hotel so they could continue shopping. They went into a bridal gown shop and looked at several dresses. Leela didn't know what she wanted but knew that when she saw it she'd know, and she eventually found it in the very back of a rack of clearance dresses.

It was perfect with its long sleeves with lace on the top and the outward flow of ruffles at the waist. It didn't have a train and that was fine with Leela, she was afraid she might trip over something like that. When she tried it on they all agreed it was perfect. When she found a beautiful veil to go with it, Leela was thrilled. It was all just perfect.

By four they had their wedding dress shopping over with and they all went back to the hotel to rest and get cleaned up for dinner. The women planned on going to a nice restaurant - they were there to have fun, and they intended on doing so. All were in agreement that Leela needed some fun after what she had been through.

That night they all got dressed up in nice dresses and took a rented car to *The Light House*. Leela wanted to go there because that was the place where she and clay had gotten engaged. Dinner was great, and afterward the ladies decided to go back to the hotel bar for a few drinks.

They got there a little after nine o'clock and there was a band playing. They had fun dancing with each other and they all had more than enough to drink. Several men had asked all of them to dance, and they all politely declined.

By one in the morning they were stumbling up to the room, where they made it as far as the front room before passing out on the two couches, still in their evening finery.

Sometime during the night they had all made their way to the bedrooms, and it was nearly eleven the next morning before the exhausted women crawled out of bed. Room service was ordered, and one by one they each got in the shower. It was almost one in the afternoon before they were ready to leave their room. The plan was to attend a play at three, and then head out of town towards home. The play was wonderful, and they talked about it all the way to Virginia. Alex was home when they got there and Leela said hello to her brother before leaving. Patricia drove the rest of the way home. When they got there Leela was exhausted but happy to see Clay.

Leela went back to work on the first of September, and Sammy was happy to have her back. She was getting big with her pregnancy and couldn't wait as many tables. Sammy was afraid that it might be awkward with Leela losing her baby, but it wasn't. Leela felt better to be filling her days at work and her life had gotten pretty boring sitting at home. The doctor told her work was a good remedy for boredom and her blood tests were still the same. Neither better nor worse, which was fine with Leela.

September flew by and the next thing Leela knew it was October first, and Leela was getting married on the fifteenth. She had the flowers ordered, the catering on track, and everything else seemed in order. Ryan was going to be the ring bearer and a daughter of one of Clay's close co-workers was going to be the flower girl. Everything seemed to be in place. Clay was planning a honeymoon in Hawaii and Leela was thrilled, she could hardly wait.

Leela had gone to see her vampires that day and let them draw her blood. That evening when she got home she had a message on their answering machine from Paulina at Dr. Risinger's office. It was quarter till five so she dialed the number.

"This is Leela Jacobs, I'm returning Paulina's call." The receptionist put her on hold, and then quickly returned.

"Ms. Jacobs, Paulina is on the other line but asked me to have you come in tomorrow morning for an appointment. Can you make it at seven A.M.?" Leela agreed, feeling nervous. She wasn't sure what this could be about. When Clay came home she told him about the call and he assured her that it would be okay, although deep down he wasn't sure himself.

The next morning Clay and Leela drove to the doctor's office together, Clay had wanted to go in case it wasn't good news.

"Leela, it's nice to see you again," Dr. Risinger said in a relaxed tone, seeing the tenseness of his patient. "How are you feeling? Any blackouts, dizzy spells, anything else out of the ordinary?" Leela shook her head. She had felt great for weeks now.

"Once again, Leela, I am shocked to say that you're back to stage one. I don't know how you do it, little lady, but you're getting better again." Leela's jaw dropped and Clay jumped with glee, hugging her.

"Oh my gosh," was all Leela could say.

"Were going to do blood draws once a month now. I don't think it's necessary to do it weekly anymore. The miscarriage must have thrown your blood work off. Just take it easy and call me with any symptom relapses." She agreed and Clay drove her to work.

Everyone at the diner was thrilled to hear about her progress, especially since she was getting married in two weeks. That night she and Clay went to dinner to celebrate.

She had already called Alex and Laura, and they were thrilled at the news. It was just what Leela needed to hear before she got married, and that would end up being the last day she had to take the antidepressants.

Chapter 26

The morning of Leela's wedding everything looked spectacular. The flowers were perfect, the decorating were beautiful, and all the ladies looked great in their dresses. The men all looked very handsome and dapper in their tuxedos, as well.

Leela sat in Patricia's old bedroom looking at herself in the mirror. "I am the luckiest woman in the world," she whispered to herself.

"Yes you are," Alex said from the door. He had been standing there admiring her. Leela blushed.

"Leela, you look absolutely beautiful and I hope this is the happiest day of your life."

Leela looked at her brother.

"Thank you, Alex. It is." They walked to the kitchen where they would prepare to walk down the aisle.

Leela couldn't believe it was time. One by one she saw her bridesmaids and the groomsmen walk down the aisle in front of her. Laura had walked alone because Alex was walking Leela - since their father wasn't able to. After watching all of her friends pass down the aisle in their finery, she heard it. The bridal march, it was finally time.

"Ready?" Alex said as he offered her his arm.

The walk down the aisle seemed endless for Leela. She focused on Clay standing right in front of her and how joyful he looked.

When Alex handed Leela's hand to Clay he kissed her on the cheek and whispered he loved her, and Leela was wrought with emotion. The reverend performed a wonderful ceremony that came to a close all too soon. Before she knew it Leela said "I do," and they were pronounced man and wife.

Everyone applauded, laughed, and cried. They all were so happy for this beautiful and unlikely couple.

"Well, Mrs. Leela Warner, how do you feel?" Clay asked her after their first kiss as husband and wife.

"Like the luckiest woman in the world," she said, and they kissed again.

The reception went well, they had the same band playing that Laura and Alex had and they sounded were good. Everyone danced and drank wine on the back lawn of Mrs. Warner's home, and by nine o'clock the crowd was starting to thin out.

Ashley, Laura, and Patricia had dragged Leela into the pool house to give her a special gift from them. They had four tiny bags sitting on the table, each labeled with the name of one of the women.

"Open it," Laura said as they each picked up their gift bag. Leela opened hers and found a beautiful charm bracelet. They all had one, and each was identical. There was a charm in the shape of Washington D.C, a charm with each of their names, as well as a lovely best friend charm. There were plenty of spaces left along the bracelet's length to add more, one each for every new adventure this little group of best friends planned - and promised - to have together. Leela thought it was wonderful, embracing each of them with tears in her eyes. They put on their bracelets and went back to the party.

By midnight they all went their separate ways. Leela and Clay were leaving bright and early the next morning so they said their goodbyes as the reception wound down.

That night Clay made love to Leela for the first time as his wife. It was loving and passionate, and a night neither of them would ever forget.

Their flight to Hawaii was long and exhausting. Leela hated flying and her nerves were wrangled the entire flight.

When they finally landed it was all worth it, Hawaii was more beautiful than she had imagined.

When they got to their hotel, The Waikiki, they were very impressed with their room. It was the honeymoon suite and everything about the room embodied love. There was an ocean view from the balcony as well as a hot tub. It might have been October but it was incredibly warm, so they also had the beach.

It was mid afternoon when they reached their room and it was a four- hour time difference from home, so it was late back in the Carolinas. They decided to stay in their room and order room service for dinner and get some rest, they had been up late the day before and wanted to do so much.

Room service was very good, and afterward Leela decided she wanted to watch a movie in bed, and Clay thought that was a great idea. He had no intentions of actually watching the movie, and as it started he began touching and caressing his new bride. With pleading eyes he asked, and so the two made love with the movie totally forgotten. he started rubbing her all over and they made love. The clock beside the bed read ten PM when they finally drifted off to sleep.

The next day they got up early and ordered breakfast from room service. Leela wanted to go explore the island and Clay was excited. They got dressed and left the hotel. They weren't sure where they wanted to start, so they just walked down to the beach. It was beautiful and they walked for what seemed like hours before finding a secluded spot to stop and sit.

They talked about how beautiful their wedding was and what they wanted to do during their six days on the island. The rest of their day was spent on a boardwalk with several outdoor shops. Leela bought some beaded jewelry for the girls back home and Clay bought the guys shot glasses.

They went to a pig roast for dinner and had a blast.

Leela learned how to Hula dance and Clay laughed at her in a grass skirt. They ate and drank and danced until neither of them could walk, and it was quite a challenge getting back to their hotel room.

The next few days went by in a blur. They lay in bed making love, went to the beach and took long walks. They visited several shops and ate at various restaurants. Clay took surfing lessons as Leela took more hula-dancing lessons. They had never had more fun.

They took a sailing trip on their fourth day there and went scuba diving as well. They did so much shopping that they had to go buy an extra suitcase to take everything home. The two filled an entire memory card with pictures, and in every one Leela looked happy and at ease. For the first time in months his wife was happy and relaxed, and Clay was thrilled. He was sure the trip done them both them good.

It was their last day in Hawaii when Leela had her first episode since the miscarriage. They had just made love and as they lay in bed she passed out. Clay had thought she'd just fallen asleep but when she woke up an hour later she was sure it was due to her condition. She told him so and they decided to take it easy. It had been a full week and they did everything they had wanted to. The next day they got on a plane to go home, happy and tan.

When they got home, Leela and Clay felt good. They had so much fun in Hawaii that it was almost boring to be back home. Leela had to go back to work the next day and so did Clay. He was going to have to go out of town following week for a week-long convention, so Leela was going to hang out with Ashley while he was gone. She wasn't upset he had to go, she knew it was only for a week and he would be back home. Plus, he was her husband now. She would follow him about anywhere.

Their first week home went by fast. Clay had a lot of catching up to do at work and Leela made dinner every night for him. She had gone to the doctor that week and had been assured the episode in Hawaii was an isolated one, because her blood work still looked fine.

When Clay left for his convention in Texas Leela was sad. She hated to see him go, especially right after they had gotten married, but he promised to call twice a day and that he'd be home on the first flight he could Friday night. She loved him so much and was glad she had finally overcome her reservations about him - and living with her condition.

The week went by slowly. Much slower than the previous two had gone. Ashley came over every night with Ryan and they made dinner and watched movies. By the time Clay got home Leela was tired of TV.

"I missed you so much!" she cried as he got off the plane.

"I missed you, too," he answered. That night they ate take-out and went straight upstairs to made love. It was as if they couldn't get enough of each other and they'd been apart months instead of a week. They fell asleep in each other's arms and slept that way all night.

That weekend Clay and Leela decided they wanted new furniture and went shopping for it. Leela wanted to change the color scheme in the living room and Clay told her she could have whatever she wanted and she wanted to make it more cheery. She found a bright blue and yellow sectional she loved, with a cooler built into the armrest for Clay. She picked out a recliner that matched, and a coffee table. Before they knew it the weekend was over and it was time for them both to go back to work.

Chapter 27

Time flew by after the wedding and before they knew it Thanksgiving had arrived, and Alex and Laura were coming to town. They were going to have dinner with Laura's family during the day and then go to Clay's mom's house that night. The next day Leela wanted to have all their friends over and make another dinner for them as well. After all, she felt she had a lot to be thankful for.

The day after thanksgiving her home was full of friends. There was Alex and Laura, Patricia and Ed. Ashley, Ryan and a new guy she'd been dating. They sat around the table and Ed said grace.

Before they started eating Alex stood up.

"I have an announcement to make," he said proudly. Laura reached to stop him but he had already said it.

"Laura is pregnant." Everyone congratulated them. They were all chatting about it when Clay noticed Leela was quiet. He realized it must be hard on her, but she seemed to hide it well. She was happy for her brother and his wife and she wished them the best.

After dinner Laura found Leela in the kitchen cleaning up.

"Leela, I'm sorry about Alex's announcement. I really wanted him to tell you in private. I know this must be hard on you." Leela looked at her sister-in-law.

"Laura, I'm happy for you. Yes, it is a bit sad for me but that doesn't mean you don't deserve it. I am thrilled to be getting a little niece or nephew." Leela meant it, too. The next best thing was Alex having babies. She thought she could be a great aunt.

They celebrated that night with lots of champagne. Laura of course drank sparkling cider and they were sorry when the night had to end.

That night in bed Clay couldn't help but notice Leela looked a bit down.

"Leela, would you like to try again?" He didn't have to say what he meant. She knew. The truth was they really weren't trying not to conceive, she just assumed she couldn't get pregnant again. She shook her head.

"I don't think I can take it again, Clay. I'm sorry." He held her tight that night, knowing it was hard on her. They slept peacefully as Leela dreamed of babies.

By Christmas time Ashley announced that she was engaged to her boyfriend, Mike. Christmas was once again a festive time at the Warner household. Leela made it a point to cook for her friends again and Alex and Laura again came to visit. After all, Laura's parents were in Palmside and not in Virginia. Clay had gotten Leela a beautiful necklace and Leela had gotten him a new suit and wallet. He had needed a nice one for his conferences.

The holidays made Leela tired but she was feeling better. Her blood tests were still great and she hadn't had any episodes lately. On New Year's Eve they had a party at the Warner house and everyone attended. Laura of course didn't drink any wine or champagne but Leela had enough for them both.

They were all having fun when Alex announced that their baby was a girl and they wanted to name her Leigh Anne. Leela almost choked on the wine she was sipping as she heard it. She looked at Alex with wide eyes.

"That's Mom's name; that is what I was going to name my baby before I lost it..." and then she realized she had said too much. Alex was staring at her and he didn't know what to say. Everyone was quiet. Laura looked almost hurt, but knew Leela had drunk too much wine. She knew it was going to be hard on her and tried to convince Alex not to dwell on it too much.

"Leela, you never told me that," Alex said to her defensively. "How did you expect me to know?" Alex was upset that Leela had snapped at him.

"Maybe I didn't get the chance to, Alex. I was robbed of it!" she snapped back. Laura and Clay looked at each other.

Clay had never seen Leela like that before. "Leela, maybe we should go get some rest," he said to her as he took her hand.

She shrank away from him. "I'm not tired. I'd like to know what else Alex has planned for his baby," she said sarcastically.

Alex had just been pushed to the edge by his sister, and couldn't hold back as he retorted, "Don't expect the rest of us to keep our joy to ourselves, Leela, just because you cannot be happy for us."

Leela was crying as she looked at him. "Well, dear brother, thanks for being so insensitive to my loss. I am thrilled that I can watch all your dreams come true - while mine wither away and die!"

Clay had heard just about enough, so he took her by the arm and led her to the bedroom where he insisted she lay down. To his relief she passed out right away from too much wine. He came downstairs and found everyone sitting quietly at the kitchen table.

"I'm so sorry," he said to Alex and Laura.

"No, Clay, she just had too much to drink and I knew this was going to be hard on her. We shouldn't have made such a deal out of it," said Laura with a bit of grace. Clay shook his head. It wasn't right what she said but he didn't know what else to say about it.

Alex didn't say anything to apologize. As far as he was concerned his sister was being selfish and outlandish. She should have been able to be happy for their good fortune, instead she was jealous - and he thought that was wrong of her. Laura had tried to explain to him that she couldn't help it, but Alex wouldn't listen.

Half an hour later everyone left, no longer in a festive mood. Alex told Clay they were going home the next day and that he didn't plan on calling Leela until she apologized. Laura assured Clay that they had all had too much wine and things would be fine, but Alex insisted it wasn't. Then they were off, with Patricia, Ed, Ashley, and Mike following shortly after. Clay was left alone to think about what had happened.

The next morning Clay woke up early and cleaned the mess up from the night before. Leela had slept till almost eleven and when she got up she was just as defensive as she was the night before.

"Are they gone?" she asked. He knew she meant Alex and Laura.

"Yes," was all he said. He thought she had overreacted the night before and had been rude.

"Good," she replied, being just as short. Clay started to say something to defend them when he realized it wouldn't do him any good.

It was Sunday and Clay was going to go visit his mother, and Leela told him she didn't want to go, so he went alone.

When he got home around three, she was sitting in the den reading a book.

"Do you think we should talk about last night?" Clay asked her. Leela didn't even look up.

"No, there is nothing to talk about." Clay thought that was pretty childish of her since her issue was with her brother, not him.

"Leela, come on now. Last night got out of hand. I know this is hard for you, but you knew they were going to have a baby sooner or later. What is wrong with you?" Leela looked up, disgusted.

"I can't, Clay. That's what wrong with me! When he told me that he wanted to name the baby after mom, the same name I had decided on, it hurt. It hurt bad, and no one will ever understand how much!" Clay was upset.

"Leela, that was my baby, too, we lost, not just yours. If you hadn't even told me about the name of the baby, how was Alex supposed to know? If he had he might have chosen something different. Don't you realize that this is hard on me, too? You're not the only one that lost that baby, Leela."

She looked up at him with tears in her eyes and said, "Well, if it is that hard on you, then maybe you deserve someone who can give you what you want."

Clay was so livid at her comment that he decided that replying wouldn't be a good idea. He just turned around and walked out of the den without saying anything more. That night they both ate in silence and went to bed without speaking.

Chapter 28

Monday morning Clay left for work without saying goodbye to Leela. As far as he was concerned she had crossed a line that weekend, not only with her brother but himself as well. Leela cried when she woke up and found herself alone. She knew that he was mad, but felt that she only spoke the truth.

That morning she went to the clinic and had her blood drawn, then picked Ashley up for work like she had for the past six months. Ashley got into the car and just said hi to Leela and nothing more. She wasn't sure if Leela had called Alex or not, but knew that she was upset because she wasn't saying much either.

Work was busy and they didn't get a chance to talk, so on the way home Ashley decided to ask. "Leela, how are you? Are you okay? You were a little upset Saturday." Leela decided not to broach the subject with her and just told her she was fine. Ashley, however, knew better.

When she got home Clay had left a message on the machine that he was working late. She took a long bubble bath and was sitting in the den reading when Clay came in around seven. "Hi," he said to her. She decided she was going to give him the cold shoulder. She was still hurt at what he had said the day before and leaving that morning without saying bye.

"Hi," she said back without looking up. He realized she wasn't going to budge so he got into the shower. By nine they were both in bed lying side by side, but not saying a word to the each other.

The next week was much the same. They had conversations when they needed to but avoided any emotional subjects. She was slowly slipping into a depression and Clay thought his wife was being ridiculous; it had been five months since they lost the baby. That weekend Clay told her he had to go out of town the following week and she just nodded. She preferred not to get into a conversation with him. It had been a week but she was still upset.

Clay was growing weary of the silent treatment and told her as much Saturday afternoon. Although she acted as if she didn't know what he was talking about, she continued to stay silent. That night Clay had attempted to take Leela out but she said she didn't feel like it.

On Sunday he told her she was still being childish and if she decided to grow up she had his cell number. He was leaving for Texas the next morning. Even that didn't faze her, and that night in bed when he reached to pull her clos she just turned away. He had been patient for too long and was finally getting irritated and he told her as much he lay there staring at her back.

Clay left town Monday morning without saying a word to Leela. She called in sick that day and stayed in bed. She wasn't feeling so good. She had slept off and on all day and when the phone rang at six-thirty that night she didn't answer it. The answering machine kicked on and she heard Clay's voice telling her he missed her and to call him when she got in. She started crying. She wasn't sure what had gotten into her but she suddenly started to panic. What had she done? She had upset not only her brother and probably Laura, too, but she had upset Clay. She wasn't even sure now why she had.

Leela didn't feel any better the next day and called in sick again. Ashley had called her three times that day, worried about her, but once again Leela didn't answer. She stayed in bed for the second day in a row and cried all day long. She once again didn't answer when Clay called that night. She hadn't talked to him since he told her she was being childish on Sunday night.

Wednesday she didn't even bother to call in sick but slept all day. The phone rang several times and she just listened on to one message after another. Clay called several times, too. He sounded frantic but she didn't flinch. Ashley also called several times and Laura called once. She said how worried she was and wished Leela would call her. Leela knew Laura had every right to hate her and felt like she was outside herself as she listened to all the messages and the ringing phone.

Leela had fallen into such a deep depression she hadn't gotten out of bed the whole week. She hadn't eaten and never answered the phone. Ashley and Patricia had come by several times and knocked on the door but Leela didn't answer it. She had become so weak from not eating that she couldn't have gotten up if she had wanted to. On Friday night around eight Clay came running through the door worried sick. He couldn't leave the conference and had been so concerned he had called everyone to check on her - but no one had been able to see her. When he walked into their bedroom and saw her lying on the bed looking thinner than ever and pale, he gasped.

"Leela? What happened?" But she didn't answer. She couldn't. She wasn't even sure if she cared that he was standing in front of her just then. Clay tried several more times to get a response out of her then decided he was taking her to the emergency room. When he tried to move her she was so hot, feverish, and limp that he called 911 instead.

An ambulance was there within minutes and they told Clay she had a fever of 105 degrees, and that her blood sugar was dangerously low. They told him she was very close to being comatose.

When they got to the hospital she was taken immediately to the intensive care unit and the doctor asked Clay how she had gotten so bad. Clay had explained to the doctor about Leela's fight with her brother and then him, how he had left town for the conference and couldn't get a hold of her, and about her depression due to her condition and the baby.

The doctor was angered that she had gotten this bad and nobody had seen her in a week. Clay tried to explain that several times someone went to the house but the doctor dismissed it. It occurred to Clay after he had been there an hour that he should call someone. At the moment he didn't know anything to tell them so he decided to wait.

Around eleven o'clock the doctor came to see him and told him that they had her on fluid and antibiotics. He told him that she was in critical condition and could only be seen every hour on the hour for fifteen minutes. Clay thought that was absurd but the doctor said it was ICU policy.

The doctor let Clay go in and see Leela, and she looked horrible. She had tubes going in her nose and IVs in her arm. He kissed her forehead as she lay sleeping. "Leela, I am so sorry, baby. I love you so much and I never should have left you like that. Please, baby, wake up." She stirred, opened her eyes, looked at him, and then shut them again. She hadn't said a word or even tried to. It was like she had given up - and that was exactly what she had done.

When Clay's fifteen minutes were up, he went to the waiting room and called his sister. She was horrified and told Clay she'd be right there, but he insisted she just wait until morning. He then called Alex and was shocked at the response he received from him.

"She's in the hospital huh?" Alex said, unconcerned. "Hope she feels better soon," He had a hardness in his voice Clay had never heard before.

Then Laura got on the phone. "Clay, I'm so sorry, Alex is still upset. What is wrong with her?" Clay gave Laura the details and hung up the phone. He promised to call the next day with an update that Alex insisted wasn't necessary. Clay couldn't believe Alex was just going to sit by with his anger after he was told his sister was in critical condition in the ICU. Laura was in Virginia scolding Alex at the same time Clay had thought it.

The weekend went by before Leela actually woke up. The doctors had been pumping fluid and insulin into her to get her hydrated and normalized, and it was like her body was resisting it. On Sunday night Leela was awake when Clay came back for his fifteen-minute visit.

Clay had tears in his eyes as he looked at her. He felt that it was all his fault for being so hard on her. "Hello, baby. Oh how I've missed you," he said as he kissed her cheek. She couldn't even smile.

"I love you," she whispered, unable to say more. There had been a tube down her throat for days and it had made her throat hurt.

"I love you, too. It's okay, baby. We're going to get through this," he said to her, but to his surprise she shook her head no.

"Alex mad at me?" she asked. He knew he was, but chose not to tell her. He shook his head no. Leela saw right through him, though, and tears sprang up in her eyes.

By the end of the following week Leela had gotten her strength back and was transferred to a regular room. Clay was relieved; he was tired of living out of a waiting room. She had started to talk to him more but was still very withdrawn. She was seeing a psychiatrist named Dr. Ally on a daily basis. Dr. Ally told Clay that she was making progress, but the depression would take a while to come out of. She explained to Clay that Leela had actually let go of herself and had withdrawn so far that she would have to fight to get back.

During the hospital stay they had monitored her condition closely. It had gotten worse again and she had once again deteriorated into stage two. Clay was just glad it never got worse. Leela was in the hospital for two weeks, and when she was finally released to go home she was still quiet. Clay took that week off of work, he wasn't leaving her alone again until he knew she was better. Leela had asked about her brother repeatedly and Clay always put her off. He had called Alex several times but he kept refusing to speak to her. Clay was frustrated and thought they both had acted like children.

By the end of the first week home Leela made progress. They were having normal conversation and she seemed to be happy at times. It was the end of January and her birthday was the second week of February.

"Do you want to take a trip for your birthday?" Clay asked on his last day home from work.

"Maybe," was all the answer she would give.

Leela made love to Clay that night for the first time since the holiday blow up, and when they woke up Monday morning she seemed almost normal. She made him breakfast and kissed him goodbye. She wasn't going to work so promised to answer his calls. Patricia was coming over at lunchtime to visit, as a favor to Clay.

Monday night Leela picked up the phone and dialed Alex's number.

"Hello?" Alex said as he answered his phone. At first Leela didn't say anything. "Hello?" he said again. He was just about to hang up when Leela spoke.

"I'm sorry, Alex," Leela said. He was quiet for a minute.

"Leela, I'm not ready to forgive you. You hurt me when all I wanted was your support and happiness. You put a dark cloud over my joy of my having a girl and threw a ridiculous fit about the name. I hope you're happy now. Laura refuses to let me name the baby after mom and it's all your fault. It meant a lot to me, too, Leela. And now I cannot have that because it will hurt your feelings. God forbid you wind up in the hospital again." He was hateful when he said it and she didn't say anything on the other end. All she could do was cry.

"If I want to talk, Leela, I'll call," he said before hanging up.

Clay was furious with Alex for treating Leela like that. He had no right to patronize her, and it could only made Leela's recovery harder. Clay was determined to get her back and he worked like hell to make her happy again. By her birthday Clay was sure he had succeeded.

Chapter 29

Clay took Leela for a weekend in Tampa Bay. They had a good time and did a lot of relaxing. Leela had seemed like her old self by then and had planned on going back to work after they got home. Clay had been trying to talk her into quitting but she refused. As long as Sammy would keep her, she was staying. It was their last day in Tampa when Clay looked at her and brought up a subject he'd been dying to bring up.

"Leela, let's adopt a baby." Leela looked at him hard.

"Clay, I have so many problems. Do you think that's smart?" Clay didn't care.

"I think you'd have to work on taking better care of yourself, honestly, And probably quit your job to be a mother, but I think it is a great idea." Leela looked thoughtful for a moment.

"We can check into it when we get home," she said to him. It wasn't a commitment but enough for him.

They drove home on Monday morning and they both took the day off, so they called a lawyer friend of Clay's and she promised to send them some information through the mail. That night Leela made dinner for him and they ate peacefully.

The next few weeks flew by. Clay worked long hours and wasn't home till almost seven, and Leela spent her time after work reading in the den. Ashley was caught up in her new fiancé Mike and they didn't do much outside of work anymore.

Leela read over the papers the lawyer had sent them on

adoption and found it very interesting and complex. They could find a pregnant mother they liked and then hope the mother would like them. Or they could adopt a baby or toddler or even an older child from a group home or foster care. Leela was sure she wanted a newborn, but the more she read on the older children the more her heart went out to them. There was one little girl in particular Leela kept coming back to in the information packet from foster care.

It was March before they knew it and Leela still hadn't spoken to Alex. Laura had called her several times and Leela had apologized to her immensely. Laura had told her several times not to worry about it and that Alex would come along. Their baby was due in July on of all days their anniversary. Leela hoped Alex would come around by then because she knew she'd want to see the baby.

In mid-March Leela told Clay she wanted to go to the foster care home and see the little girl she had read about. She hadn't been able to get her out of her head, she was four years old and was very petite - just like Leela. She had light brunette hair, brown eyes, and fair skin - again, just like Leela. Clay was intrigued by her photo and agreed they'd make an appointment. On March 25th Leela and Clay drove to Hansen City, South Carolina to meet Annabelle Renee.

The group foster home was very nice. Leela had a fear it would be old and run down and the kids would sleep on mattresses on the floor like you'd see in movies, but the house was beautiful on the outside and inside and it was surrounded by a large yard with swing sets.

Erin Smith met them at the front door and showed them to her office on the first floor. She explained to them that children were brought there when they weren't adopted or regular foster homes could not be found. She explained there were too many unwanted children in the world just begging to be loved.

Erin then gave them a tour. They saw the infants and the toddlers before going to the wing with children from ages four to eight. Each room consisted of two beds for kids and one adult bed. They walked into the room at the end of the hall and Leela immediately saw Annabelle sitting on her bed holding a teddy bear. Annabelle looked up at her and Clay with her big brown eyes and smiled. She held out her hand and introduced herself, which she seemed to have practiced. That broke both Clay and Leela's heart. She was such a sweet girl, and very smart for her age. They took Annabelle out to the swing sets and they played with her all day.

After taking Annabelle back to her room, they followed Erin to her office. "Would you two like a minute alone?" she asked. Clay looked at Leela and could tell she already loved the girl. He shook his head.

"Actually, I think we'd like to start the adoption process." Leela squeezed Clay's hand. She was sure that was what she wanted.

They spent an hour filling out paperwork. They of course had to have a criminal background check done on them. Leela had been very up front with Erin from the beginning about her condition and had supplied statements from Dr. Risinger stating Leela had progressed back to stage one and was doing better. Erin told them it was not a problem and assured them she'd file the paperwork as soon as possible.

Two weeks went by before they heard back from foster care. They had been approved to take Annabelle home by the court and the adoption would be final in six months. Leela told Sammy she could no longer work at the diner and all Sammy could do was hug her, telling her she understood.

That weekend Leela and Clay went out and bought a whole new bedroom suite for Annabelle's room along with enough toys to fill another room. They had made her bedroom the guest room next to the master suite and her toy room in the workout room downstairs. Leela had bought several outfits and hung them in her closet. They were so excited - everyone was excited for them. Patricia, Ed, Ashley, Mike, and Ryan were going to come over the next weekend to meet her. Laura was happy for them, too, but Alex was still being stubborn, and Clay's mother was thrilled she was finally getting a granddaughter to dote over.

That Monday they drove to Hansen City again and Annabelle was waiting for them with a big smile at the front door, with all her belongings packed into two suitcases. She gave them big hugs like she'd known them her whole life, and Leela and Clay already felt a love for the child like she had always been theirs from birth

Clay had taken six weeks off of work, taking advantage of a program his work had that encouraged adoptions. The first week they spent adjusting Annabelle to her new home. She seemed happy and was very good at following the simple rules that Leela had explained to her. Leela in turn learned what Annabelle liked to eat and what she didn't. She learned what she was afraid of and what she liked to play with. In no time at they were all like a happy family, and Annabelle was already trying the words "mommy and daddy" on for size.

The get together that weekend was a hit and Annabelle got to meet her Aunt Patricia and her Uncle Ed. Clay's mother quickly became Granny warner, and Ashley suddenly found herself being called "Aunt Ashley." She and Ryan quickly became fast friends, and they played outside on the swing set and in the playhouse together. The only thing missing was Laura and Alex. Leela thought about calling them, but she didn't want to ruin the day for Annabelle if they made her new mother sad.

Everyone loved Annabelle and said she looked just like them. She was smart, and showed everyone how she could write her own name and say her ABCs. She was also quite proud she could count to ten and she did it over and over again for her daddy.

Clay kissed Leela on the cheek as they watched their

new daughter count off on her fingers. They couldn't have been happier.

Chapter 30

The next two months flew by and it was almost time for Laura to have the baby. She was coming back to Palmside to have it since her family was there, and she hoped her stubborn husband would finally go see his sister. Leela had sent them pictures of Annabelle and Laura couldn't wait to meet her. She was determined to see her whether Alex would or not. Alex had told her the child looked like his sister, and was happy for them, but he had said it without conviction.

They arrived in Palmside on July twentieth, and as Laura got settled in with her mother, Alex told her he was going to take a drive. She secretly hoped it was to his sister's, but wasn't sure. He had been so preoccupied lately.

Alex drove up to his sister's house and parked in front. He slowly walked up the driveway and heard laughter in the backyard, so he walked around the house and stopped as he saw Leela pushing a little girl on a swing. The girl looked like a much younger version of his sister, and they both were laughing as the swing swooshed through the air.

The moment he saw her all his anger began to dissolve. He had missed her so much and realized how stupid he had been to not see her in the hospital. Leela didn't see him standing there, so he just stood there quietly and watched.

Both brother and sister were shocked when Annabelle spied him and squealed "Uncle Alex, mommy!" Leela had turned in wonder at the direction Annabelle had pointed, and saw her brother. She had shown her daughter pictures of Alex, but hadn't expected the girl to remember him so well. Alex himself was a bit shocked.

Clay, who had seen Alex pull up, sat silently at the back window to watch the scene unfold. As Leela walked slowly toward Alex holding Annabelle's hand, she was at a loss for words. She wasn't sure what to say.

"Hi, Uncle," Annabelle said. Alex looked at Leela and smiled, then he stooped down to Annabelle's size and smiled at her.

"Why hello there, cutie." Annabelle instantly put her skinny little arms around Alex and hugged him. He hugged her right back and then picked her up. With Annabelle in his arms, he hugged Leela.

"I'm sorry, sis," he said. And with tears in her eyes she hugged him back. Clay was smiling out the window, relieved.

Leela called Laura at her mom's house and told her Alex was there and asked her to come over for dinner to meet Annabelle. Laura said she'd love to and Leela was shocked to see her when she arrived. Her belly was huge and she looked oh so very pregnant.

That afternoon was a dream come true for Leela. She had her husband, daughter, all her friends and thankfully her brother back. Everyone had a good time as Clay grilled chicken and Laura sat underneath the shade tree with Leela. She was due any time and was eager to have the baby. Alex was playing with Annabelle in the playhouse and the women smiled at the sight.

"He's going to make a great father," Leela said to Laura as they laughed. Alex had to bend down to walk through the house.

"Laura, did you guys decide on a name yet?" Laura shook her head. Alex still wanted to name the baby Leigh Anne but Laura was trying to discourage him from it.

"Not yet," she said.

"I think, if Alex still wants to, that Leigh Anne would be the perfect name for your baby girl." Laura smiled at

Leela and Leela smiled back. The two women had a connection like they were blood sisters - not just in-laws.

"Thank you, Leela. I'm sure Alex would appreciate your approval. It means a lot to him." Leela looked at Laura with tears in her eyes.

"It would mean a lot to me, too," she said, and then women hugged.

Annabelle ran to Leela and jumped in her lap and Alex walked to the grill. "Mommy, Uncle Alex said he's having a baby. Is he?"

Leela and Laura laughed. "Actually, honey, Aunt Laura is having the baby. See, it is inside her tummy but it will come out soon." Annabelle looked confused as she studied Laura's belly.

"Okay," she said, not completely satisfied with the answer. She jumped off her lap and ran toward the guys.

"She is such a cutie," Laura told Leela.

"Yes, she is, and she is everything I have ever wanted," Leela replied, and she meant it.

Dinner that night was a happy event. Alex and Leela got along great and Leela told Alex that she hoped he would still name his baby after their mother. Alex hugged his sister and told her he would.

After they finished dinner, Alex stood up.

"I have an announcement to make." Clay and Leela looked at each other. Alex had said those very words twice before standing in that very same spot. The first time was to tell them about the baby and the second was to tell them what they planned on naming the baby. Clay was a bit nervous but Leela just smiled, looking anxious.

"Laura and I are moving to Palmside," Alex said with a wide grin. Leela was so happy to hear that. She jumped out of her seat and ran over to Alex and hugged him. She was so glad, especially with the baby coming so soon.

Laura was smiling from ear to ear as well. Her whole family was there and so was Alex's, so it just seemed right. Clay was happy, too.

"Wow!" Leela said as she sat back down. "What about your jobs?" she said to both of them.

"Well, I'm quitting my job. I'm just a secretary and Alex's firm has an office in Marino. It's only a fifteen-minute drive from Palmside. So we'll be moving as soon as we find a house." Leela couldn't have been happier. Clay told Alex he had a friend who was a realtor and Alex promised to call him the next day.

Annabelle had been sitting in Clay's lap and was almost asleep. She had a big day playing with her Uncle Alex and she was tired. Leela picked her up and Alex, Laura, and Clay all kissed her cheek good night before Leela carried her up to her room and tucked her into bed.

That night they sat around the table and talked about upcoming plans. Laura and Alex were staying in town until the baby was born, which should be within the week. During that time Alex would be setting up his new office and looking for a new house. Then, after the baby was about two weeks old, they would go back to Virginia and start packing up their house. They had started weeks before but still had some to do. They were hiring a moving company to do all their moving; all they had to do was pack it up. During the time they'd be in Palmside they would be staying with Laura's parents.

Leela told Laura that she was more than welcome to spend her days with her since she didn't work anymore. Most of the time she and Annabelle spent their time in the backyard playing and getting dirty. Laura thanked her and told her she would love to.

After Alex and Laura left to return to her parent's home Clay and Leela went up to bed. Leela was so happy they were moving, finally things were starting to go right for her.

The next day Ashley and Ryan were coming over to play. They had weekly play dates on Sunday afternoons. Leela told Ashley about her brother coming over the day before and how they had made up. Then she told her about them moving to town and Ashley couldn't have been happier for her.

"That's great!" she said.

Leela and Ashley sat under the tree watching the kids on the swing set. Ryan was so good with Annabelle and she thought the world of him. He treated her like he would treat a sister and Leela had to smile at that.

Alex and Laura were spending time with her family but were going to come over that evening after they had dinner. Leela had invited Ashley and Ryan over for dinner as well and told her of course she could bring her fiancé Mike, and Ashley accepted. Then she called Patricia and Ed and they gladly accepted as well. Her guests that night were not only her best friends but her family, too.

Dinner went well. Annabelle and Ryan played together as the adults sat and finished eating. Leela prepared a special meal for them because she knew Annabelle didn't like the fish she was cooking for dinner. The kids had hamburgers, macaroni and cheese and apple sauce. They loved it.

Alex and Laura arrived just in time for dessert. Leela had made apple pies and a chocolate cake, and they all ate until they groaned. Laura had told Leela that she thought the baby would come any minute, and she was starting to feel her drop. All the women were so excited; it was all they could talk about. The men, however, watched a baseball game in the living room.

Leela had bought something for the baby weeks before, not knowing if she'd ever get to give it to them, but she knew now was the perfect time. She told the ladies she'd be right back. First, she went to the toy room to check on Annabelle and Ryan, and they smiled at her as they played with Lego blocks. Then she went upstairs to her bedroom and pulled a box out of the closet.

When she walked back into the kitchen with the box, Ashley knew what it was. She had been with her when she bought the contents.

"Laura, I've gotten something for the baby. I've had it a while but wasn't sure when I'd get to give it to you." Laura smiled.

"Oh, Leela, you didn't have to." But she took the box and opened it.

Inside were several items. First, was a beautiful newborn white dress that looked a lot like a Christening gown. Then there were several onesies and sleepers in various girl colors, and at the bottom was a baby book to record all the memorable moments in the baby's life.

"Oh, Leela, it's so beautiful," she said, holding the gown in one hand and the book in the other. Leela hugged her.

"I'm sorry it took so long to get it to you." The ladies then talked about the baby for a while longer and then Ashley announced she had to get going because she had to work in the morning. Patricia and Ed finally had to take off as well, but Alex and Laura stayed.

Leela put Annabelle to bed at eight-thirty and the four of them decided to play some cards. They played for a few hours before Laura started to yawn.

"I guess it's getting late," Alex said regretfully, but he knew that Laura needed her rest. Leela knew that Alex would be at his new office the next day getting things set up to move.

"Laura, if you're not busy tomorrow, why don't you come over for lunch." Laura agreed and then they left.

Chapter 31

Monday morning Clay kissed Leela on the cheek before leaving for work, but didn't wake her up. She had told him she felt sick before going to bed and Clay was afraid she was catching the flu. That was the last thing she and Annabelle needed. He checked in on Annabelle and kissed her on the cheek as well. They were both sleeping so peaceful.

Leela woke up at nine o'clock and she felt sick to her stomach. She ran to the bathroom and almost didn't make it. She kneeled at the toilet for five minutes before she was done vomiting. She was trying to do it as quietly as possible so she didn't wake Annabelle up.

When she did check in on Annabelle on her way downstairs, she was still sleeping. She went to kitchen and found the coffee already made and helped herself to a cup, but as she brought it up to her mouth to take a drink she instantly felt sick again. She ran to the bathroom downstairs and vomited again. She was having second thoughts about having lunch with Laura. If she was sick she didn't want to give anything to Laura with her baby was due any day. Within the hour Leela felt better. Whatever had upset her stomach seemed to be gone, and she was thankful it was. When Annabelle got up around ten-thirty she seemed fine, and not to be affected by the flu.

Leela made a ham salad for lunch and when Laura showed up around noon she looked even bigger than the day before.

"I know it has to be soon," she told Leela as she waddled into the kitchen.

They sat in the backyard and had lunch while Annabelle ate in her playhouse she loved so much. Leela and Laura talked about the baby, as usual, and then about what Laura was looking for in a house. There were several in the area for sale and the women were planning on going to look at them that afternoon while Alex got things settled at his new office.

Leela had forgotten about her flu symptoms she had had that morning and felt just fine now as the ladies and Annabelle drove from house to house. Laura found something she didn't like about all four they saw. The backyard was too small or the bedrooms were too small. She wanted something comparable to the one she had in Virginia, which was very similar to Leela and clay's home.

They headed back to Leela's after the fourth house. Sitting in the car wasn't very comfortable for Laura and Annabelle was getting anxious in the back seat. Right before they turned onto Leela's street, a "for sale" sign caught Laura's eye.

"Hey, go back that way!" Laura said. Leela turned the car around and saw the house Laura was talking about. It was a beautiful big house with a huge yard and the "for sale" sign was new. Leela knew that she hadn't seen it the day before.

She pulled up in the long driveway lined with bushes and they all got out. They walked around the house and found a man working in the back yard in the garage.

"Oh, I'm sorry, sir. We were just looking at the house. We saw the 'for sale' sign," Laura explained, as he looked shocked to see them.

"Oh, no problem," he said, "can I show you the inside, then?." They nodded and he took them in.

"This was my grandparents' place and they were just placed in a nursing home last month. We can't afford to keep the house so we're going to have to sell."

Leela thought it was a sad story but Laura loved the house. It had two bedrooms, a bathroom, a kitchen, dining room and living room downstairs and three bedrooms and a bathroom upstairs.

"This is perfect, Leela!" Laura said as they finished the tour of the house. "I love it. Will someone be here tonight so my husband can see it?" she asked the man.

"My wife will be here between five and seven. Will that be okay?" Laura nodded her head yes, smiling from ear to ear.

"What are you asking for it?" Leela asked. The man shook his head.

"Well, honestly, we are in a hurry to sell it because we have to pay for the retirement home, so we are asking well below market value. It can be yours for one hundred thirty thousand dollars." Leela couldn't believe her ears. It was a lot cheaper than she had been expecting. All the other houses they had looked at were almost two hundred fifty thousand.

"That's great!" Laura said, trying to hide her excitement. "We'll see you at five-thirty." As they climbed back into the car Laura looked at Leela. "I want that house." And Leela was sure she'd get it.

When they got back to Leela's house it was almost three-thirty. Alex promised to be there by four, and Laura couldn't wait to show him the house.

Alex loved it. He told the owners he'd put an offer on it and would pay them the asking price without a haggle. After all, it was a steal. And they agreed that Alex and Laura could move in immediately after closing the loan, which, after a quick call to one of Clay's good friends in the banking business, was set for three weeks.

That night they all ate dinner at Leela and Clay's to celebrate. They grilled steaks on the grill and Leela and Laura made the rest. It was a festive evening as they celebrated one step closer to moving, but after dinner was finished Leela felt weak again. Laura noticed she was a bit pale but when she asked her Leela said she was fine. Everyone always worried about her. The last thing she wanted was them stressing over the flu.

Laura held her stomach most of the night. She was having little cramps that her doctor said was just the baby stretching and getting ready. She was ready to have this baby and was hoping it would come soon.

As they gathered outside under Leela's favorite tree to relax after dinner, Laura doubled over with pain.

"Oh!" she yelled. Alex came running.

"Honey, are you okay?" And just as she yelled her water broke and they all stood staring at her in amazement. It was time.

"It's time!" she said to Alex as he went inside to call her doctor. Leela set Laura down in a chair and told her to time her contractions. They were seven minutes apart but Laura was in such pain when she had them that Leela told Alex she thought they should head to the hospital, so they did.

Leela and Clay drove separately and dropped Annabelle off at Ashley's house. A hospital was no place for a child of her age even if it was the maternity ward. Ashley told her she'd keep her overnight and to give Laura her love.

When Clay and Leela got to the hospital they already had Laura in a room hooked up to monitors and an IV. They had checked her and she was only three centimeters dilated, telling her she had to be at least five before they'd give her an epidural. She was in such pain that when the contractions came at the five-minute mark she was squirming and yelling. All the breathing that Leela tried to get her to do wasn't helping.

After an hour of what Leela thought looked like pure torture, the doctor checked Laura again and told her she was finally five centimeters and could have her epidural. Clay and Leela walked out of the room so the doctor could give it to her.

Leela looked almost as exhausted as Laura did.

"Are you okay, love?" Clay asked her. "You don't look so good." Clay was always worried about her relapsing into her condition.

"Yes, I feel fine. I'm just tired, is all." In truth Leela did feel weak. And her stomach was upset. And she was from time to time getting dizzy.

When they went back into the room ten minutes later, Laura looked much more relaxed than she had before the epidural.

"I guess that really works," Leela joked with Laura, who was adamantly nodding her head in agreement.

"I'd recommend it to any woman," Laura said back.

They sat in Laura's room for six hours, waiting, and when it finally came time Clay stepped out of the room. Laura had asked Leela to stay and Leela had been touched. To their surprise the baby came after just ten minutes of pushing, and before they knew it there was a beautiful little girl. Leela was amazed as she watched her mother's namesake take her first breath.

Within seconds of being born Leigh Ann let out her first wailing cry. They all laughed when she did. She was perfect with ten finger, ten toes, and a head full of bright blonde curly hair. She looked just like Alex had as a baby.

When Clay joined them again he was amazed at her, too. She was so precious. Looking at Alex and Laura she could see they'd never been happier. Leela felt a slight pain knowing that was a feeling she'd never have, holding her baby in her arms for the first time. But she now had Annabelle, whom she loved just as much. She was just so happy for her brother.

It was past midnight when Leela and Clay got home. Leela was exhausted and Clay was, too. It had been a long emotional evening and they both fell asleep right away.

Chapter 32

Leela was up at six o'clock with Clay the next morning. She felt horrible. Her stomach was upset again and she was in the bathroom vomiting twice within the first thirty minutes of being up. Clay had heard her and was concerned, but she assured him it was just the flu. Clay asked her to go see a doctor, anyway.

She felt better by the time she had to go pick up Annabelle and was even in good spirits. She told Ashley about the baby and how perfect she was and Ashley could tell that there were no hard feelings about her. She was genuinely happy. That afternoon before her doctor appointment she took Annabelle to see the baby.

Laura and Alex were doing well and were happy because they got to bring the baby home that night. Laura was going to stay at her mother's house and soon Alex would finish packing up their old home so they could move to their new one.

After leaving the hospital Leela and Annabelle headed to Dr. Risinger's office. "Leela, I am very happy with your progress. Your condition is practically in remission. How have you been feeling?" Leela told him about her flu symptoms in the mornings but how she felt better the rest of the day. Then she told him about the periodic dizzy spells and how she'd been tired lately. The doctor looked at her suspiciously and told her he wanted to do a quick blood test.

Twenty minutes later the doctor came back into the room.

"Leela, I'm gonna have Paulina take Annabelle out of the room for a minute." Leela nodded and was instantly concerned. It must be bad if they didn't want Annabelle to hear what he had to say. Paulina took Annabelle by the hand and asked her if she wanted to see her fish. Annabelle nodded and went with her.

"Oh my god, Dr. Risinger, is it that bad?" Leela said with tears in her eye. All she could think of was she was worse again and that she was going to die, leaving behind Clay and Annabelle and the rest of her family.

"Actually, quite the opposite, depending on how you look at it Leela," he replied. She was confused now.

"I don't understand," Leela said. She really didn't. She was clueless.

"Leela, your fine. You just happen to be pregnant," he said and she looked stunned. She had been in this situation before but she had never expected it again.

"Are you sure?" She wasn't sure whether to be happy or not, and was quickly becoming scared.

"I'm positive. Just like your pregnancy test," he said jokingly, trying to lighten her mood. "Leela, you know the risks. You're not waitressing anymore. Your life is much less stressful. You have a better chance now of having a successful pregnancy, and we can watch you like a hawk. This, Leela, is a good thing. This is what you've been wanting." He was trying to convince her.

"Thank you," she said, still in shock. She was still in shock as she collected Annabelle and drove home.

Clay was home from work when she pulled up in the driveway. How would she tell him, she wondered to herself. Annabelle ran up to him and jumped in his arms. He was a good father. He loved Annabelle very much, and he loved Leela, too.

"Hey, honey, see the baby today?" Leela nodded. Clay saw that she looked upset and thought it was because of the baby, hoping she wasn't getting depressed again.

"Are you okay?" Leela looked at him and shook her

head no. "Annabelle honey, why don't you go out back to the playhouse and we'll be around in a minute." Annabelle kissed her daddy and ran out the back door.

"Leela, sit down. What's wrong?"

Leela looked at him and in a low, flat voice said, "I'm pregnant."

Clay didn't think he heard her correctly and said, "What'd you say? I didn't hear you."

This time she looked him in the eye.

"Clay, I'm pregnant again."

Clay looked as stunned as she had in the doctor's office.

"Wow, Leela, are you sure?" Then he shook his head. "I'm sorry, of course you're sure, you went to the doctor didn't you. That's great, baby," he said, but deep down he was worried something would go wrong.

"What will we do?" she asked.

Clay laughed.

"Leela, this is a good thing, not a death sentence." As he said that he immediately wished he hadn't. "What I mean is we'll get through this, honey; we'll be careful and in the end we'll have us a baby. Annabelle will be a big sister." Leela smiled. She had tears in her eyes. Of course this was a good thing. She just had to keep thinking that way.

That night they decided not to hide anything this time. They would invite all their closest friends over for dinner the next evening and announce it. Leela was excited. She was worried as well, but promised herself that she was going to do this right and come out of it with a baby.

That night they lay in bed side by side, holding each other and talking about their future, Annabelle, and the pregnancy. They both fell asleep still holding each other.

Leela spent all day getting ready for the coming evening. She had a roast in the oven and vegetables cooking, too. She was so excited that she was going to announce her little secret tonight that the morning sickness she had didn't even bother her. As far as she was concerned it was welcome as long as it didn't get any worse.

Ashley, Mike and Ryan arrived first. Ashley could tell something was up because she was glowing. But when she asked about it Leela told her to hold her horses, she'd find out with the rest. Patricia and Ed arrived next and they all sat in the backyard waiting on the new baby. Laura, Alex, and baby Leigh Ann arrived thirty minutes later. Alex joked about how they had to take their whole house with them now that they had a baby to pack around. It wasn't too far from the truth.

They set up a playpen in the den so the baby could sleep, and even brought the baby monitors so they could hear when she woke up. They brought cans of formula and several diapers, wipes, and changes of clothes. Leela was suddenly aware of how much work having a baby was.

Laura looked good for just having a baby, and you could tell they were tired but happy as can be. They were all wondering why they were called there that night, and no one would have guessed.

They gathered around the dinner table and passed around platters filled with food. When everyone was finished eating Alex looked at her.

"Okay, sis. What's going on?" Clay went to the kitchen and brought out wine glasses for all of them and poured a very expensive wine into them. He handed all of them a glass.

"I'd like to make a toast," he said, smiling widely. "First, I'd like to thank all of our friends who are here. You are our closest friends and we love you all. I'd like to toast Annabelle, for one, who is our blessing. Then I'd like to propose a toast to Leigh Anne who is the most beautiful baby I've ever seen. May she stay healthy and grow up to be a beautiful woman like her mother. And when I say she's the most beautiful baby I've ever seen, I actually mean until mine is born eight months from now."

It took about fifteen seconds for everyone to catch what he said. He and Leela were grinning from ear to ear as they saw all the surprised looks on their friends' faces.

"Oh my god!" Ashley said.

"Congratulations!" Laura said, crying and hugging Leela. Everyone was shocked and happy.

"We just found out yesterday," Leela said. "So besides the doctor, you all are the first to know." There were a lot of tears and hugs going around the room. It was a night to remember.

The next several months flew by. Leela went to the doctor every two weeks and got a clean bill of health for herself and the baby. Alex and Laura moved into their new house just around the corner from them, and Ashley and Mike started to plan their wedding that they set for the following August, three months after Leela was to have her baby.

When she was five months pregnant and they had found out her baby was a boy, Clay had been thrilled, as was everyone else. Annabelle was just as excited as everyone else that she was getting a brother. She was getting used to having Leigh Anne around and Leela thought she'd would be fine with a new baby brother. The doctor told her she was doing remarkably well, and that as long as she kept on doing what she was doing, this baby would come with no worries.

Finally, on May 29th, at five thirty-two in the morning, Clay Alexander Warner was born. He was seven pounds and twenty inches long, and as Leela held him in her arms for the first time, she cried tears of joy. She finally had what was forbidden for so long. She had finally learned the power of love. She finally had her baby.

About the Author

Jenny Leigh Jones is a romance author and workout junkie living in Southern Indiana.

When Jenny isn't writing, pounding out the weights, or doing a workout, she enjoys spending time with her husband Bob, their children, and her dog Daisy Girl.

Jenny and Bob keep a Demon locked in their garage, and on weekends they like to let it out to get a little exercise on the race track.